The Red Velvet Murders

Sharon Hendryx McDaniel

PublishAmerica
Baltimore

ISBN: 1-60836-484-4
PUBLISHED BY PUBLISHAMERICA, LLLP
www.publishamerica.com
Baltimore

Printed in the United States of America

Synopsis

Detective Jeremy Lottle had been working on the same case with no leads for four long months. When his Captain recruited a psychic to help him out, he knew that he was headed for trouble. In the first place he didn't believe in psychic abilities and he sure didn't want to be seen with an old gypsy looking, crystal ball toting, tarot card reading hag, he would be laughed right out of the station house.

Allison Kramer was not the old hag that Jeremy had envisioned, she was tall, slender and blonde with the most incredible blue eyes he had ever seen. But the thing that bothered him the most was that she held a striking resemblance to the two dead women in the case that he was trying so desperately to solve.

Allison Kramer does prove to have some psychic abilities but when it comes down to her own life being in danger she doesn't have a clue. Can Jeremy save her before she too becomes a victim of the Red Velvet Killer?

The Red
Velvet Murders

Prologue

"I think your starting to get a little to close to this creep, maybe even starting to like him." Jeremy accused Allison.

"That's absurd, I'm just trying to help you do your job, and I want to get this guy behind bars as much as you do, if not more."

"There was a time when I believed you wanted to catch him, but now I'm not so sure, your trail has grown cold all of a sudden."

"I don't know what to tell you, I just haven't had any vibes lately." She said throwing her hands up in the air.

Jeremy snickered. "Vibes…. I knew this was a mistake, I told the Captain that this wasn't a good idea, but he insisted that you could help. Do you want to know what I think about your psychic abilities?" He stared at her.

"No, but I'm sure your going to tell me." Allison flopped down in the over stuffed chair against the wall a few feet from his desk.

Jeremy turned his back then circled to the other side of the desk to face her.

"I think it's all a load of crap, I think your only here to be near me, I think you've wanted me since the first day you saw me." He threw his ink pen down on the desk and waited for her response with his arms crossed.

Allison felt her jaw drop. "What an ego you have, I never knew you existed until the day we met in your captain's office, and even you can't deny that it's because of me you even have a clue who the killer could be." She stood up walked to his desk and poked him hard in the chest. "You should be grateful." She added before grabbing up her hand bag and turning towards the door. Stopping suddenly, a smile crossing her face, she turned around to find that he had moved and was standing right behind her. She couldn't help but notice his wide muscular shoulders which only made her more angry at him and herself, she wasn't here to find romance, she was here to find a killer. Before she knew what she was doing she kicked Jeremy in the shin as hard as she could and quickly ran for the door.

Jeremy bent over in pain, damn her, why would she do that? Was she five?

"I'll get you for that." He called after her. "Bitch!." He added under his breath. Unknown to either Jeremy or Allison, Captain Johnson had been listening and watching from his office door.

"What's all the yelling about?" The captain asked.

"Why don't you ask your psychic friend out there." He waved his hand to the front office where he saw another detective had stopped Allison before she could make the final escape from the station, she was watching him while pretending to be listening to what the officer was saying to her. "I told you she was going to be trouble." Jeremy sat down pulling up the leg of his jeans so that he could see how much damage Allison had done. His leg was swelling and he could see the start of a nasty bruise. It might not have hurt so bad if she hadn't been wearing those shit kicker boots, he hated those things. The captain found the whole situation between the two of them humorous but who had time to laugh, they needed to find the killer before another woman was killed and Allison could help.

"As I recall detective, when I brought her into this case you had no leads at all and now…thanks to her, you at least have some leads to work on, they sound like good ones too. I think you owe the lady an apology."

"Ok, so she gave us a description of the guy which could fit half the city but now the trail has grown cold, she claims she can't get anymore vibes."

Jeremy looked up from his bruised swollen leg, the captain had a silly grin on his face.

"What?" Jeremy demanded to know.

"I don't think this case is the only thing bothering you."

"I've been thinking about nothing but this case for the past six months Captain." He rubbed his shin again.

"She's a beautiful woman."

"Who?" He acted as if he didn't know who the captain was talking about but he knew full well it was Allison, it was always Allison. Yes he thought about her all the time, but he was not about to admit that to anyone."

"Allison, she's a looker."

"So what's your point?"

"Just that she's pretty and I think you like her."

"She's a hell cat, look at my leg, she did this to me."

Captain Johnson stuck his head outside the office and yelled for Allison.

"Get in this office right now." He ordered as if she were on his payroll.

The entire room of officers and detectives watched as she made her way back to the office she had just fled.

"Sit down." He ordered.

Allison did as she was told, even though she didn't like the idea of occupying the same space as detective Lottle. She found the man rude and obnoxious from the very first day that they had met and nothing had changed, he was impossible to work with, it was no wonder that he had never been married. What woman in her right mind would have him? When she first saw him she thought that he was handsome and might be nice to work with, but then he opened his mouth and reality hit, he'd been impossible from the very first day and he obviously was not going to change.

Allison had taken a seat next to Jeremy and when she looked down and saw the goose egg she'd left on his shin she couldn't help but giggle.

"Now the two of you had better listen up, I want this nonsense to stop, your acting like two children, it's way past time for the two of you to start working together as a team, once we find this maniac and put him away the two of you can kill each other for all I care."

"Maybe he's retired." Jeremy mumbled, slouching deeper into his chair.

"He hasn't stopped he's merely been forced to take a break, he knows that we are onto him." Captain said.

"I've been trying to use my powers to get in touch with him— "Powers." Jeremy interrupted. "Give me a break, you don't have any Powers, especially psychic ones. Get in touch with this lady."

He grabbed his crotch and watched as Allison's face turned crimson.

"Show some respect detective or I'll throw you out on your ear." The Captain warned. He should have known Lottle would come up with something rude like that, he was embarrassed for the man.

"That's all right captain, I can handle detective Lottle." Allison smirked.

"Handle this baby." Jeremy grabbed his crotch again, laughing.

"You should be careful what you wish for detective Lottle, it just might come true." Allison approached him and placed her hand on his crotch, her caress prompted a smile but it was only a second before her light touch became a tight squeeze. "From now on I expect to be treated with the same respect that you show for your other co workers and the respect I have shown you for the past few months, is that to much to ask for detective?" She tightened her grip.

"Nooo." He squealed.

Allison released her hold.

"Great. Now that we have established the fact that Ms. Kramer can handle herself—and you, can we please get back to work? That goes for the rest of you as well." He yelled out to the dozen or so on lookers that had gathered to see the show.

"I'll be leaving early today captain, but I will be here first thing in the morning, can't wait to see you detective." With that said, Allison threw her bag over her shoulder and sashayed out the door….again.

One

Detective Jeremy Lottle stood over the lifeless body of nineteen year old Stacy Peebles, her blonde hair splayed out like a fan over the old ratty brown carpet of her dorm room floor. It was one week before Christmas and most of the college students had headed home for the holiday break, but not Stacy, she had decided to stay at school, things were not so great for her at home these days, her father had recently remarried, her new stepmother was only three years older than herself and needless to say, they didn't get along very well. Stacy knew that Her step mom was only there for her fathers money but it was useless for her to tell him that, he was smitten and there was nothing she could do to change that, he would have to figure that out himself and once he did Stacy would go home and forgive him as she often did when he put other people or business in front of her. She just hoped that he didn't lose his fortune before he figured out what a gold digger he had really married. But now it would make no difference to her because sometime in the middle of the night some one had come into her dorm room and strangled her to death.

Detective Lottle bent over the body and gently closed the eyes of the dead girl her blue eyes had been frozen in time, the horror she felt as she realized that she was dying had shown in them. Jeremy couldn't begin to imagine how she must have felt to wake up in the middle of the night and find a stranger or even some one she possibly knew and maybe even trusted in her room ready to take her life so easily. Was it a man? A jealous lover perhaps? Or was it a jealous woman? He wondered to himself. He looked over the girls body once more, she was wearing a bright red bra with matching panties.

"Keeping in the holiday spirit." He said aloud.

"What did you say ?" Asked Captain Johnson as he entered the room.

"Nothing, I was just thinking out loud."

"Does it look like rape?"

"No. No obvious signs anyway, but we have to wait for the medical examiners report to know for sure."

"Do you know who this girl is ?" Johnson asked.

"I heard some one say her name is Stacy Peebles."

"Stacy…as in the daughter of Tony Peebles?" Captain questioned.

"Tony Peebles, isn't he the filthy rich computer wiz from Delano?" Jeremy asked.

"Yes, he is very rich."

A uniformed officer came into the room to confirm what they had suspected.

"She is the one and only daughter of Tony Peebles." The officer informed Them." As he shook his head in disbelief.

"Well Lottle, do you think this murder has anything to do with who her father is?

"Some one wanting to settle a score possibly? It's worth looking into Cap."

"I suggest you look into this one real deep, poor kid, she didn't deserve this."

"I look thoroughly into every murder Cap, because no one deserves this, doesn't matter if her Daddy's rich or not."

"I didn't mean it the way you took it Lottle."

Jeremy took one more look at the girls young pretty face before pulling the sheet up over her head. He silently promised to make whoever was Responsible for her death pay for their crime.

He went out into the hall to question the few people who had stayed in the dorm for the holiday, just as he suspected no one had seen anything or heard anything at least they weren't fessing up to it if they had. So with that part out of the way, now came the hardest part of the job, he would have to make the dreaded call to the family. In this case the dreaded visit. Tony Peebles only lived 30 minutes from where his daughter now lay dead and the deceased at least deserved to have someone tell her father in person that she had passed away. No, that someone had taken her life, his only child's life, it was beyond him how someone could look into those crystal blue eyes and slowly choke the life out of her.

Sometimes he hated his job, but when he had a perpetrator in custody and knew he had one more criminal off the street it sure made him feel good.

Jeremy put his note pad into his shirt pocket and set in for the thirty minute drive ahead. The highway was all but deserted, there weren't very many people driving around at two thirty in the morning.

When he reached the house of the Billionaire Peebles he noticed that there were lights on inside. As he reached the front door he could hear voices, loud angry voices, he wondered if someone had not already notified them by phone. He would have some ones badge if that were the case.

As he'd walked up the long narrow side walk he noticed the immaculate landscaping along the way, just as he reached for the doorbell a young woman appeared in the doorway, she was tall, brunette, wearing a thin white t shirt and very short shorts, Jeremy found that odd, it was after all the middle of winter, California or not it was still rather chilly to be headed outside in that kind of attire. Where ever she was going she seemed to be in a big hurry, she stopped short when she saw him.

"Jeees, you scared the hell out of me." She held a hand to her chest as if to Stop herself from having a heart attack.

"Sorry." He apologized. He disliked this woman immediately.

"Who are you anyway?" She demanded to know.

Charming woman—he thought to himself. "I'm detective Jeremy Lottle." He held his hand out to her but she didn't take it, instead she looked over her shoulder back into the house. "I can't believe you called the cops on me, Your such an ass." She told the man.

"No one called me Miss."

"What?" She turned her attention back to Jeremy.

"I didn't call the police." Tony Peebles appeared in the doorway.

Jeremy recognized him from the countless pictures in the newspapers. However he always looked strong and proud in the media but tonight he just looked old and worn out. Jeremy was sure it had a lot to do with his lovely new bride.

"The neighbors probably called." Mr. Peebles guessed.

"No, they didn't."

A worried look crossed Mr. Peebles face.

He held his hand out once again. "Detective Lottle."

The man didn't accept his hand shake either but he did step aside and invite him into his home.

"Is this about my daughter?"

"Yes sir, it is."

The man sighed deeply. "I was afraid that she might start acting out after I married Teresa, the two of them haven't been getting along."

"You know I tried with that spoiled brat—Teresa started.

"That's enough." Tony stopped her. "I thought you were leaving me."

"I was, but now I'm interested in what kind of trouble your daughter has gotten herself into." She lit up a cigarette and took a long drag. Blowing smoke directly into her husbands face.

Jeremy said nothing yet, he was hoping the man would insist she leave the room but apparently he didn't care if she stayed or not.

"Ok detective, lets get on with it." He prompted.

Jeremy cleared his throat. " Your daughter Stacy, was found strangled in her dorm room." Straight to the point, after all there was no easy way to tell a man his daughter had been murdered.

"What? Are you sure?" He stood up and then sat back down.

"Yes sir."

Mr. Peebles dropped his head, there were no tears but Jeremy could see the sorrow on the mans face, possibly he felt some guilt over it, maybe he had chosen his selfish young wife over his own daughter and now that she was gone he had no chance to patch things up. He felt sorry for the man. Jeremy looked around the spacious living area, there were no pictures of Stacy anywhere, but there was an over abundance of photos of the new Mrs. Peebles. Teresa, he recalled her name. What a witch, he thought. She was standing by the sliding glass doors that overlooked the back yard, Jeremy could see her reflection in the glass, was that a smile on her face? He believed so, what kind of heartless woman would be happy that her husbands only child had been murdered? Unless she had something to do with that murder. He would have to check into her and what she had been doing that night. But he would do that another time, when the old man wasn't around.

Jeremy stood up from his seat. " Mr. Peebles, I am truly sorry for your loss and I will do everything in my power to find out who took your daughter from you."

"Why don't you start with that bitch over there." He motioned to his wife.

"Do you have reason to suspect Teresa?"

"Stacy always warned me about her just wanting my money, I wished I had listened sooner, my daughter could see right through her."

"Don't worry, I fully intend to be back to question Mrs. Peebles."

As they walked to the door Jeremy noticed tears in the old mans eyes.

He had come to the conclusion that Teresa Peebles was not a woman he would ever like but for the old mans sake he hoped she had nothing to do with Stacy's murder. Mr. Peebles took Jeremy's hand in his and thanked him for having the decency to deliver the news in person. " A lesser man would have just called on the phone, it proves that you care." He told him.

"I do care Mr. Peebles, and feel free to call me anytime day or night if you have any questions or if you think of something that might be significant to the case."

"Can I ask you a question detective?"

"Sure."

"Do you think that Stacy's murder might have something to do with me? With my business...could my daughter have been killed by some one trying to send me a message, could it be my fault that she is dead?"

"I'm looking at all possibilities Sir, right now we don't have any suspects."

"I see, thank you detective Lottle."

With that said he shut the door. Jeremy sat in his car outside the hillside mansion for at least an hour before heading back to the station, he couldn't seem to get the picture of Stacy's dead body out of his mind. He had a feeling this case was going to give him trouble, a lot of trouble.

Two

Allison Kramer sat upright in bed, a fine bead of sweat covering her upper Lip. She threw the covers off of her and stepped out of bed, walking groggily to the bathroom bumping into the wall and then lifting her leg high to step over the pile of dirty clothes she had left in the middle of the floor. She felt like the ball in a pinball game being bounced all over the place, she swore softly. If she weren't such a slob those clothes would have already been laundered and hung up instead of still lying on the floor in a heap.

Now standing in front of the bathroom sink she closed her eyes and washed the sweat from her face. She'd had bad dreams but for the life of her she could not remember what she had dreamt about. She reached blindly for a towel and patted her face dry, when she opened her eyes she gasped, it was not her reflection that stared back at her, it was similar, the hair was the same length and color, the sparkling blue eyes stared right through her, she jerked around expecting to see the intruder but there was no one there, when she turned back to the mirror she saw only her own reflection again. Creepy, chills ran down her spine, however With Allison Kramer it wasn't unusual to experience something like that.

She walked back into her bedroom and sank into the fluffy mattress knowing that she would not sleep the rest of the night because when Allison saw that girl in her mirror she knew it either meant that the girl was in trouble or worse, the girl was already dead, and she wanted Allison's help to find the person responsible for her death.

Allison Kramer had what some people called a gift but to her it was more of a curse, she wasn't the kind of fortune teller or tarot card reader that you could find on almost any street corner these days or the kind you found at carnivals she wasn't a fake that was out to take peoples hard earned money because people were so desperate for some one to tell them that their family member from the other side is standing next to them and had a message for them, not to say people didn't come over from the other side but usually when a dead person visited her it was because they could not get to the other side with out her help, usually their death was unexpected or suspicious and their soul could not rest until it was settled.

Allison was more of a closet psychic, meaning she didn't want people to know she had any kind of insight to the dead, people didn't like to believe it was possible. She had even worked with the police on a few occasions, crimes that they couldn't solve, not to say that the police were inferior but sometimes they just needed a little extra help, it was true, sometimes the dead did indeed communicate with Allison Kramer, this is why she had very few friends. It had been this way for her growing up and still in adulthood, people just did not want to associate with someone they felt was, well for lack of a better word a nut case. Allison tried to keep a low profile but the last case she helped the Los Angeles police with had turned into a circus, the media had been all over her, practically camped out in her front yard, that made her neighbors real happy. But it didn't matter because the most important thing was that the case ended in a good way, the two teen aged girls that had been abducted were found alive and unharmed thanks to her Skills and insight.

The alarm buzzed in her ear it was time for her to get ready for work, she'd hoped for a little more sleep but hadn't gotten what she wished for so now she would just have to make the best of the day. Allison didn't usually consider herself a morning person but once she opened the door to her pet shop every morning and was greeted by the birds and the kittens and the adorable puppies all or at least most of her troubles would go away at least for a while. But this morning as she opened the door to Pet Crazy she could tell immediately that there was something wrong, there were no cheerful mews from the kittens and no songs from the birds and once she reached the counter she realized why, some one had broken into her store, they had slammed the register down on the floor in an effort to get it open, they must have been furious to find it empty. She looked around and saw that none of the animals were hurt and she quickly went back outside and called the police from her cell phone. It seemed like an eternity before they finally arrived. Actually it had only been five minutes, there was one squad car and one unmarked unit, she watched as a tall slim young man in uniform climbed out of the squad car and a slightly overweight middle aged man climbed out of the unmarked vehicle.

"Ms. Kramer?" Asked the older man.

"Yes." She held out her hand to him and he shook it vigorously. His hand was sweaty and when he turned to look at the younger officer she quickly wiped the sweat from her hand on her jeans.

"I'm Captain Johnson and this is Officer Sampson."

"It's nice to meet you both." She acknowledged the younger man but he seemed disinterested in her and the whole reason that he was there.

"Have you touched anything inside?"

"Just the door knob, but I looked around and it doesn't appear that they've taken anything, but the animals are pretty upset."

The younger cop snickered, she didn't appreciate it.

They stepped into the shop and the captain reached over to pet a beagle pup on the top of his head. " Cute little fella."

"His name is Henry." She offered.

Johnson looked at her oddly. " Do you name all your pets before they are purchased?"

"Yes, and I like to think of them as adopted not bought."

"Doesn't that confuse them when they are….adopted and their name gets changed?"

"Oh, animals can adjust to a new name right away."

"I see, so you know a lot about animals Ms. Kramer?"

"I learn more every day, one thing I do know is who ever was in here last night scared these animals."

"But none of them are hurt, it looks like the only motive here was money, my guess would be some teenagers, possibly even druggies looking for some cash to make a buy."

Allison didn't like the thought of some druggie being in her store and she couldn't put her finger on it but she was sure the break in had more to do with some one just wanting money.

"Captain?"

"Yes Mam."

"Do you honestly believe that this was just a random break in?"

"I'm sure that's all it is, we will take finger prints and see what we can come up with, maybe they left us something to go on."

His cell phone rang and soon he was apologizing for having to leave.

"I have to go but my officers will process the scene and I'll let you know what we find." He shook her hand and she turned back to her animals.

"Ms. Kramer, I just can't shake the feeling that I know you from some where, are you sure we have never met before?" One hand rested on his side.

"I don't think so Captain."

"But your so familiar." He knocked on the side of his head as if that would make him remember where he had seen her before. She hadn't wanted him to recognize her and she thought about not telling him anything but the poor man was going to knock himself out if she kept letting him beat on his head like that. "You've probably seen me on the news." She said quietly.

"I'm sorry." He stopped thumping on his head to look at her.

"About six months ago I helped the Los Angeles police solve a crime, luckily it didn't end in murder, the media was all over me making a big production of the whole thing."

"Are you or were you in law enforcement?"

"No, I have psychic abilities and the police asked for my help."

"Oh."

"The media had my face plastered all over the television and the newspapers, for weeks they were camped out on my front lawn, I had to move here to Bakersfield to get away from all of it."

He snapped his fingers. "That's right, you're the psychic that helped them catch the child molester, two young girls were found alive and well, thanks to you."

"Yes, Luckily we found them before he had a chance to hurt them."

But the media couldn't make up their minds, some praised her and some condemned her, accusing her of being a fraud. Some even accused her of being in on the crime so that she could be a hero. Every where she went some one was in her face, she couldn't walk out her front door with out some reporter or nutcase off the street getting in her face. The only choice she had was to move away.

"I'm sorry to bring it up, but you did a good thing."

"Thank you Captain Johnson, but there are a lot of people who feel the opposite of you and I would just like to forget about it and live in peace."

"I understand Ms. Kramer but you will tell me if you get any leads on your own case right?"

"Of course, you will be the first person I call." He pulled out a business card and put it in her hand. "I have to go now, if you have any questions just ask officer Sampson." He nodded in the young mans direction, the officer still looked like he'd rather be anywhere but there.

"I'll do that, thank you."

"I'd like to know how it works someday."

"How what works?"

"Your psychic ability."

"It doesn't always work the same way Captain, and I can't make it work at will, it just happens."

"Oh, well I would still like to talk about it someday."

"We will see what happens." She was ready for him to leave now and he seemed to pick up on that.

"Ok, good enough for now. I'm off." He jogged out the door setting the bell off as he went.

"Off your rocker." She heard officer Sampson mumble. He seemed very disrespectful and she immediately did not like the man, she was very uncomfortable around him, luckily there were two other officers there dusting for prints and she wouldn't have to be alone with him.

Three

Jeremy stood in his office fighting with his tie. "Damn thing work with me." He told it. There was a knock on the door, he turned to see Phyllis, His Captains secretary watching him.

"Can I help you with that?" She offered.

"Are you telling me that you actually know how to tie one of these things?"

She entered the room and stood in front of him, she reached up to work with the tie. "Are you kidding me, I tied my husbands tie for him every day for twenty years, right up until the day they buried him."

"I had no idea Phyllis."

"Yes, I'm sure there is a lot you don't know about me Detective Lottle." She giggled.

"Phyllis, are you implying that you have skeletons in your closet?"

"You're the detective, figure it out." She turned him around to face the mirror so that he could see how she tied his tie.

"Wow, I've been in front of this mirror for thirty minutes and couldn't figure it out."

Suddenly she reached around him and pulled the tie loose.

"Hey, why did you do that?"

"Because you need to learn how to do it yourself and I will show you how." She put her arms around him and tied his tie again while he watched closely. "Nice."

"Thank you sir, now it's your turn."

"What, come on Phyllis, can't I just come to you when I need a tie tied? It's not like I wear one every day."

"No, I only do this on a daily basis for a few select people and you—as sweet as you are, are not one of the privileged few." She pinched his cheek.

"I see how you are." He turned back to the mirror and followed the same motions that Phyllis had done moments before." It worked, he caught her reflection in the mirror, she really was a nice looking woman, for an older woman that is, he pegged her to be around fifty, maybe even older. "It looks pretty good, for a beginner." She told him.

"Thanks Phyllis, I couldn't have done it with out you."

"What's going on in here?" Captain poked his head into Jeremy's office.

"Nothing, Phyllis just taught me how to tie my own tie."

"Oh, she's been trying to teach me for years, I decided it was just easier for me to come in early every morning and let her do it for me."

Jeremy looked from the captain over to Phyllis, she was blushing just a bit. He wondered if there was something going on between them. Phyllis walked past him and as she passed the captain he reached out and slapped her on the rear end. She never turned around but he heard her giggle as she hot footed it to her desk to answer the ever ringing phone.

"That answers my question."

"What question would that be Lottle?" Captain asked with raised eyebrows.

"I was just wondering if you and Phyllis had something going on."

"No, no, just giving the gal a hard time."

"Nothing going on you say?"

"Nothing what like you're implying."

"So you wouldn't mind if I asked her out?" He bit back a giggle.

Captain stood still like he was in shell shock. "Why would you want to do that?"

"She's a good looking woman, been widowed for a few years now, I figure she might be ready to start seeing some one."

"And you think that someone would be you?" The Captain's face was red.

"Why not me?"

"How old are you son?"

"Thirty three."

"Exactly, she's fifty five."

"So, I can appreciate a hot older woman."

"She is hot—what the hell is wrong with you Lottle? Don't you have something else to do?"

"Actually I'm going to Stacy Peebles funeral."

"Oh that's today huh?"

"Yes, I feel that I should pay my respects, and it gives me the chance to check out the guests, see if anyone looks suspicious."

"Should I send a uniform with you just in case?"

"No, I wouldn't want to scare anyone off."

"So you don't have any leads yet?"

"The only person that has acted weird about the murder is the step mother, she actually seems happy that the girl is dead."

"Well Jeremy, money is all that some people care about."

"I think that's exactly what the young Mrs. Peebles cares about she thinks with Stacy out of the way that she can get her inheritance in the divorce settlement."

"Do you think she killed her?"

"As much as I despise the woman, I don't peg her for a killer."

"She could have set it up."

"That thought did cross my mind, I have already questioned her, checked all of her financial records for the past three months, no unusual activity. I have to believe she's clean."

"What about the old man?"

"I can't find anyone who has a bad word to say about the man, he's a rich business man but apparently he got his money honestly, I can't find anyone he cheated or stole from or lied to about anything."

"That is odd."

"I'm starting to think it was just a random killing not connected to family or money, just a girl who was in the wrong place at the wrong time."

"Well, whatever the case may be we still have to find the creep and put him away in case he decides that he wants to do this to another girl."

"I'm working on it captain."

"All right, if for some reason you need back up ask for officer Sampson."

"Trying to break him in?"

"Had him on a case with me yesterday and he seemed bored with it all, I think he is ready for some action."

"Them young guns always think they are ready for some action until they get it. What kind of boring case did you have him on, stolen tricycle?"

"No I used all those boring cases up on you when you were starting out, had him on a pet shop robbery."

"Sounds like fun."

"It was strange, nothing was missing but they threw stuff around and upset the animals as much if not more than the owner."

"Let me guess, a little old lady around eighty and the place was probably filled with cats and kittens."

"How wrong you are Lottle, she was a smoking hot honey about your age."

"Smokin hot honey… Who are you?" He had never heard his captain talk like that about a woman.

"I may be old enough to be your dad but I can still appreciate a fine looking young woman when I see her."

"Watch out, Phyllis might get jealous."

"There is nothing going on with me and Phyllis." He denied.

"Then you won't mind if I ask her out."

"Office romances never work Lottle."

"Your just saying that because you want her for yourself."

"And if I do….it would be none of your business."

"Yes sir." Jeremy gave him an officers salute. "I have to get going to that funeral, I'll check in later. Jeremy slowly walked out the door, he was never in a real big hurry to get anywhere but yet he always managed to get there on time. He stopped at Phyllis desk and whispered something in her ear making her blush, they both looked in the captains direction and grinned like two kids keeping a secret. Captain wondered if Jeremy had really been serious about asking Phyllis out, or was he just trying to get a rise out of him knowing that he really did have a thing for her. He really shouldn't have slapped her on the bottom in front of Lottle but couldn't help himself, the woman and her form fitting skirt, he was crazy about her, he'd finally mustered up the nerve to ask her out a while back but when the big day had finally come he'd landed himself in the hospital with a broken leg after a foot pursuit. He knew it was a bad idea when he gave chase but they had been after this two bit crook for months and he couldn't just let him get away without trying to catch him, The crook had led him down a narrow alley. The patrol car wouldn't fit so he had to give chase on foot, he radioed for backup and proceeded to chase the guy, halfway down the alley someone jumped out from behind a dumpster and whacked him in the leg with a wooden baseball bat, he went down quick knowing instantly that his leg was broke and it was, in two different places. So that evening when he should have been on a date with Phyllis he was laid up on the hospital bed with an eyesore of a cast on his leg. He hadn't asked her out again, but he had wanted to, she tied his tie every morning and made him the best coffee he had ever drank, occasionally she would bring him lunch, something leftover that she had made herself the night before. He didn't know what he had been waiting for, he stood up from his desk marched over to Phyllis and—"Will you go to dinner with me tonight?" He asked.

"Oh, Don, I wished that you had asked me sooner, I just told Jeremy that I would go out with him tonight." Captains face turned bright red not with embarrassment but with anger. "I'll kill him." He whispered.

Phyllis laughed. " Calm down chief I'm just kidding. I would love to have dinner with you tonight."

"You would?"

"Yes, I've been waiting for darn near a year for you get your nerve up again."

"Well, I'm asking now."

"And I'm accepting."

"I'll pick you up about seven then."

"I'll be ready, unless you decide to break another leg."

"That's not even funny Phyllis. But for your information I don't plan on pursuing any criminals today."

"Good, because I don't think I can wait another year for you to ask me out."

She slapped him on the backside as he had done to her earlier and promptly returned her attention to her work as if nothing had happened. Captain looked around the room to see if anyone else had seen what transpired, most of the shift hadn't arrived yet so he was sure that his secretary slapping him on the rear hadn't been seen. He couldn't wait to see what the date would bring.

Jeremy drove in circles looking for a place to park at the church, there had to be at least a hundred cars crammed into the tiny parking lot and along the street, finally he settled for a spot two blocks away, as he walked to the church he noticed all of the out of state license plates on the vehicles, he assumed they were family members. There were people gathered on the church steps when he approached so apparently the service hadn't started yet.

"Psssst, Detective Lottle." He heard from behind a bush. He leaned around to see who was calling him, he saw Teresa Peebles stomping out a cigarette and blowing that last puff of smoke into the air.

"Mrs. Peebles." He walked back down the steps to face her.

"Call me Teresa." She told him running her hand over his arm, it made him sick.

"I'm glad you came today, it will mean so much to Tony that you care."

"Speaking of Tony, shouldn't you be with your husband right now?"

"I'm headed that way now, I just needed a smoke."

"I'm sure that couldn't wait." He mumbled.

"Detective Lottle, I get the impression you don't like me very much."

"It shows does it?"

"Oh! You hurt my feelings, I bet if given the chance I could change your mind about me." "I doubt that very much." He tried to walk away from her but she stepped in front of him for the block. "I'm soon to be a very rich woman detective, and I would bet on Your salary you don't get to travel much, we could do that together…. We could drink margaritas on the beach in the Bahamas and make love in the sand."

"Do you plan on killing your husband like you did your step daughter?" She looked taken aback. "I did not kill Stacy, and I do not have to kill my husband to get half of his millions, it's amazing what a grief stricken man will agree to just to get rid of me."

"My question is why would such a smart man ever want you in the first place?"

She stood on her tiptoes to whisper in his ear. "Because I am that good—"

"Give it a rest Teresa." Tony Peebles spoke from the front steps of the church. All of the other guests had taken seats and were waiting for Tony to begin the service.

Jeremy Shook the mans hand as he walked through the double doors.

"I hope you didn't fall for anything she had to say, you look like a smarter man than myself."

"We all have our week moments sir, this wasn't one of mine."

"Good to hear it, come on in so we can get started."

Teresa tried to follow Jeremy but Tony put his arm up to stop her.

"You can sit out on the curb with the other garbage. Your not welcome here."

He shut the door in her face, turning back to Jeremy. "I'm sorry about her behavior, she wasn't like that when we first met, actually she was a good friend of Stacy's, I thought she was. Now I believe it Was all just an act, she had an agenda the whole time.

"Mr. Peebles, money makes people do all sorts of things that they normally wouldn't."

"Then again Detective. Some people are just born bad."

"That's true also."

"I'm glad that you're here detective and I would like for you to sit with the family."

"I don't want to intrude on your grief." He honestly didn't feel like he should sit with the family, however if he did, that would mean that he would be sitting behind a dark window where he would be able to observe the mourners.

"Please detective, it would mean a lot to me."

"Ok." Jeremy followed him into the family room and took a seat next to him, the seat where his wife should have been sitting if she had been any kind of a wife at all. He stared out into the sea of faces, there were people of all ages but his eyes caught a group of young girls, if he had to guess they looked like they would still be in high school, they all had on cheerleading uniforms, he found that to be odd attire for a funeral.

"Those girls your fixated on, they are McFarland High cheerleaders. Stacy was head cheerleader all four years of high school, the girls adored her, Especially Destiny Gamble, Stacy had groomed Destiny to take over as head cheerleader this year."

"It sounds like you were real involved in your daughters life."

"Stacy's mother passed away when she was only eight years old, I had to be mother and father, I tried to be as involved as possible in every aspect of her life…. Until last year when I married Teresa, she never forgave me for that, Stacy could see right through her, I was blind."

"I'm sorry you didn't get the chance to make up with her."

"Does no one any good to be sorry now, I just need you to help me find who killed her and why."

"That's what I want to Sir."

The service took two hours and the procession to the cemetery took another two hours. But he wasn't complaining because he felt that he at least owed this much to the dead girl, to be close by, just in case anything or anyone acted suspicious. They stood around the grave site while the minister said a few more words, Jeremy noticed officer Sampson standing several feet away leaning against a tree, he assumed that Captain Johnson had called him in for back up. Just in case he was needed, he watched him answer his cell phone and then he quickly left, he passed Teresa Peebles on his way to the squad car, it looked like they exchanged words but from where he was standing he couldn't make out what was said, but he wondered what the two of them could have to talk about, knowing her, or at least what he learned so far she was probably trying to pick him up. After all he was a good enough looking kid in a uniform and much closer to her own age than Tony Peebles was. Now that she was probably going to be a rich woman of course she would be on the prowl for another man.

Some people slowly started to leave the cemetery while others branched off to visit other grave sites. Jeremy headed to his car, his step slowed when he saw Teresa leaning against his vehicle, her blouse was unbuttoned just enough to show her great cleavage, her bright red lipstick looked so out of place against her pale skin, She looked like a streetwalker. He pulled his keys out of his pocket and unlocked his door. She didn't move.

"What are you doing here?" He asked.

"Since he locked me out of the Church service I figured he couldn't keep me away from the graveside service so here I am to pay my last respects."

"It's already over, and I'm not sure I believe your just here to pay your last respects."

"She was my stepdaughter and at one time we were friends."

"I guess you were her friend long enough to get in good with Daddy and then she was of no more use to you once you had his trust—and his money."

"You think you know everything about my life detective? You don't know a damn thing." She stomped her foot.

"I know enough to want you to stay away from me, unless I call you."

"That's fine, I've lost interest in you anyway. But maybe you could put in a good word to the hottie cop that just left." Jeremy had one leg in the car, but he stopped. "Are you serious?"

"Just because you turned me down doesn't mean that he will."

"Do me a favor Teresa."

"Oh now you want favors from me?" She winked at him.

"The only thing I want from you is for you to get the hell off my car and go home and wipe that lipstick off your face, you look like a two bit tramp."

Teresa jumped away from the car when the engine started. "Screw you Lottle."

"What a way to pay your last respects lady." He drove away leaving Teresa in a fog of exhaust.

Four

Jeremy drove down highway 99, his mind now on one thing only—food, he was hungry, the funeral had taken nearly all day long he'd missed breakfast and after dealing with Teresa Peebles he'd missed lunch as well so now it was almost dinner time, the Rice Hut sounded good, he could start with a nice bowl of egg drop soup and then some sweet and sour pork and a couple of egg rolls. He Didn't eat Chinese much but sometimes he did get the craving for it.

Jeremy was just about to take the exit that would get him to Rice hut when his cell phone rang, he checked the caller ID, captain Johnson, That meant one thing for sure, he wasn't going to be eating anytime soon.

"Yep." He answered.

"Where you at?"

"Just getting back to town."

"Just now? That was a heck of a long funeral."

"Yes, it was." He agreed, leaving out the part of Teresa Peebles taking up much of that time.

"We got another."

"Another what?" But he already knew what the Captain was talking about, he already had that familiar wrenching in his gut.

"Another dead girl, I'm standing over her as we speak, she looks a lot like the one you just buried today."

"Really? Same MO?"

"Looks that way, red under ware, strangled, what's your ETA Lottle?"

"I don't know where you are Cap."

"I guess you would need to know that wouldn't you?"

"It might help."

"Bakersfield college, girls dorm seven, room number six."

"You ok, Cap?"

"I'm good, just thinking about my date with Phyllis tonight."

"Really, Phyllis?"

"Gotta problem with that?"

"No, but can I just say….it's about time. I bet she was getting tired of waiting.

"ETA?" Captain asked again cutting him off.

"Ten minutes."

"Great." Click. Jeremy put his phone back on his belt holster, another girl dead at the hands of this creep. It had only been four days since he found Stacy on the floor of her dorm room now he would have to let another family know that their daughter had experienced the same fate. He desperately wanted a cigarette, he rummaged through the glove box, nothing. The center console, again nothing. He was trying to stop and was somewhat succeeding but at times like this he really had a craving for one. If he had time he probably would have stopped to pick up a pack but time wouldn't allow it so he continued onto the college. He Didn't have to look very hard for dorm seven, there was a crowd gathered in the front of it, most of them young girls, no doubt the ones that lived in that particular building, where else would they have to go while the police did their investigation. They were all probably wondering the same thing. Which of them could be next on the killers list.

Jeremy made his way through the thick crowd, he flashed his badge at the uniforms before crossing the yellow tape that separated the people from the entrance of the building. He walked down the hall, the door to room six was open, he peeked inside, Crime scene was already there.

"Get in here Lottle." Captain ordered.

"Don't you have somewhere to be?"

"Yes, but I was waiting for your slow ass to get here."

"Well, I'm here now."

"Good, I'm turning it all over to you, here's what I have so far." He handed him a note pad.

"You can either tell the family yourself or you can send a uniform to do it, I'll leave that up to you."

"Thanks."

"Don't mention it, and don't call me unless it's absolutely necessary."

"Wouldn't dream of it."

"I don't like this Lottle, I don't like it at all, I'm afraid we have a real psycho out there."

"Look's that way."

"Two young girls, both blond and blue eyed, freshmen in college. Did you see how many girls are standing out front that fit the same description?"

"Yes I did Cap."

"What do you suggest we do Lottle? Put them all under surveillance, tell them to go home to their parents until further notice? How are we supposed to protect them?

"I don't know." He snapped at the Captain.

"Find this creep Lottle and find him fast." He stomped out the door not looking back.

Jeremy turned back to the victim, her hair was splayed on the carpet just as Stacy's had been, he took the time to arrange their bodies just the same, she was wearing the same color under ware, that couldn't have been a coincidence, this was definitely not a copy cat killer, everything was almost identical. It was for sure that this was done by the same person. He thumbed through the notebook that Captain had left him, the girls name was Jill Drake, eighteen, freshman in college, her parents were David and Eileen Drake, he was a lawyer and she was a housewife with two other children still living at home Johnny age twelve and Janet age sixteen. "Great, another family he had to devastate." He said aloud to himself. He looked around the room, it was very clean and neat, just like Stacy's had been. He wondered if all college girls were so neat, he knew for a fact that college boys were as messy as they could be, he'd been there and done that. But girls? I guess he would be finding out soon enough because he was going to have to visit other dorm rooms to ask questions. He spotted something between the wall and a dresser, he pulled out a rubber glove from the csi case that was in the floor, he put it on and carefully pulled out a very slim laptop computer, that was something he hadn't found in Stacy's room. Her father had said he purchased one for her a week earlier as a Christmas gift but it was never recovered in the investigation. Since they had been on the outs he figured she didn't keep the gift from her father. Jeremy flipped over the computer and on the bottom of it was a silver label that read... To My daughter, my everything. Merry Christmas Stacy. 2008.

"Well, that explains why we couldn't find it in Stacy's room."

"Pardon" Asked the CSI.

"Nothing, here's something else for you to process, and could you put a rush on this, there may be something on that computer that could help us out."

"Sure thing Detective."

"That's a nice computer isn't it?"

Jeremy turned to the open doorway and saw a short little girl who looked like she might only be twelve years old standing there."

"How did you get past the officers outside?"

"In case you didn't notice, I'm kind of small, I sneak into a lot of places."

"What's your name?" He asked.

"Janice Deets."

"Well, Janice Deets, I'm detective Lottle." He shook her hand and she gave him a crooked smile. "Did you know Jill very well?"

"She was my room mate when school first started but—"

"But what?"

"I don't really know what happened, we got along great at first but sometime around thanksgiving she started acting different and before I could figure her out she had gotten a transfer to this private room."

"What about Stacy Peebles, did you know her?"

"I knew her, but not well, Stacy and Jill were good friends form high school so they talked a lot."

They did? So why was it that Jill hadn't come forward when Stacy was killed. He questioned so many people why was it that he missed her? She might have been able to tell him something that could have saved her own life.

"Do you know anything about that laptop?" She stepped further into the room.

"Is it ok if I come in now?"

"Yes, come on in." The scene had already been processed and the body removed. The chalk outline of Jill's body remained. Janice stared down at it. "It's kind of creepy in here isn't it?" She asked, just to make sure that she wasn't alone in thinking that.

"Yes, it is kind of creepy in here, how about we talk in your dorm room."

"Sure." Jeremy followed Janice down the hall into her room. Officer Sampson closed and sealed off the door to room number six and watched closely until Janice and Jeremy were in the other room and the door shut behind them. He knew that he should have questioned the girl in the open hallway but he didn't want all ears hearing what was said about this case. Jeremy looked around Janice's room, it was not a filthy mess, but it was cluttered as he suspected most dorm rooms would be.

"Sit down please." She picked some books up off of a chair and motioned for him to sit, he did. She plopped down across from him on the edge of her bed.

"Do you know how Stacy's computer got into Jill's room?"

"I'm not positive, but I think that she gave it to her. Jill and Stacy had been hanging out together, a lot. They seemed to always be huddled over that laptop, there was definitely something going on…we all just thought they were trying to get a jump on school work. They used to use the computers in the library until Tony gave the lap top to Stacy."

"Tony? Your on first name basis with Mr. Peebles?" He asked.

"Mr. Peebles always insisted that we call him Tony."

"Who is we?"

"Anyone that was a friend of his daughter, even if we barely knew her."

Jeremy jotted some things down in his pocket notebook. "I wonder what was so interesting in that laptop." He wondered out loud.

"I wish I could tell you." She answered his question that he hadn't realized he'd spoken aloud. "But you know, I do remember waking up in the middle of the night to the two of them arguing, when I peeked out into the hall to see what was going on Stacy shoved the computer at Jill and told her to just take it if it bothered her so much."

"What bothered her?"

"I don't know, but I don't think they spoke again after that night."

"When was this, when did this happen?"

"I think it was three days before Stacy was found."

"Why didn't you come forward sooner with this information, it could have helped me, it might have saved Jill's life."

Tears began to well in Janice's eyes. She hadn't not come forward on purpose, she would have done anything if she thought it could have saved the life of a friend. The dam broke free and now the girl was crying full crocodile tears. Jeremy felt like a heel making the kid cry, but seriously that tidbit of information could have helped at the time, but it did him no good now. "I'm sorry Janice, it's not your fault, I shouldn't have spoken to you like that, I mean how could you know that either Stacey or Jill was going to be murdered…right."

"I swear detective, if I had known it could have helped you or saved a life I would have said something sooner but the other detective I talked to told me that he would call me if he needed to ask any questions."

"What other detective?" As far as he knew he was the only one on this case, except for what little bit the Captain worked. "I don't know his name."

"Was he in uniform or plain clothes?"

"Plain clothes, but he said he was a detective and he would call me, but you know what? He didn't even ask for my name or number."

"Did you get his name?"

"I'm sorry but no."

"He did tell me not to talk to anyone else but him about the case."

"Listen Janice, I don't think that guy was a real cop."

"Why not?"

"First of all I am the only one working Stacy's case, no one else should have talked to you at all and second, if he were a real cop he would have gotten your contact information."

He handed her a business card with his numbers on it and then he asked for hers in return.

"Janice, if you think of anything else, please call me."

"I will." She promised and closed the door behind him.

Jeremy wasn't surprised to find the hall littered with girls, he was sure they were all gossiping about the murder and he even heard some whispering about what he might have been doing in the closed dorm room with Janice, he thought about walking on out the door and just going home but if there was any chance one of them might know something he figured he shouldn't pass up the opportunity to ask. "Do any of you know anything about Stacy or Jill's murders?" They all shook their heads no. "So none of you saw or heard anything suspicious tonight or the night Stacy was killed?" Once again no one was talking. He walked over to a bulletin board and tacked up his card. " I will leave this here just in case any of you remember anything that could help me"

"Or in case we can help you like Janice just helped you in her room." Someone smarted off. And some one slapped him on the butt. Of course when he turned around no one was confessing to having been the culprits. "You girls can get yourselves in a lot of trouble behaving like this." "Behaving like what detective?" Asked one of the girls who made her way through the crowd to stand in front of him in a tiny little t shirt and panties.

"Acting like hoochies is going to get you into trouble." He told them.

"Hoochies! No one says that anymore, you must be older than you look."

The other girls laughed. " I don't know the most recent slang but what ever you want to call it, acting like you are will only bring you trouble and unless you want to be on a cold slab like Jill is right now I suggest you change your attitude." The room became silent.

"That's right girls, once your dead, your dead. You Don't get to come back and have a do over at life."

"We get it Detective."

"I hope so, I really don't want to come here again and see another of you dead on the floor, or have to tell another parent that their child is dead, so all of you be careful."

By this time the girls were so ashamed of themselves that they couldn't even look him in the eye, they were staring down at the floor. Maybe they would think about what he had said. "I don't ever want to come back to see another one of you dead and I never want to have to tell another family that their loved one has been killed. By now all the girls were ashamed of themselves and the behavior that they had displayed. He was right, none of them were safe. Jeremy had no idea what this killer's motive was, why he targeted who he did and who he might target next. The only thing he knew for certain was that he was still hungry, going all day without eating had given him a headache. He hopped into the explorer and riffled through the glove box until he found a bottle of aspirin, he popped three into his mouth and chewed them up then he headed to the Rice Hut for what he hoped would be a quiet, non eventful dinner.

Five

It was midnight and Allison was up pacing the floor, she had seen in the paper about the young girl that had been murdered. Stacy Peebles, the face that peered at her from the paper was the same face that she had seen in the mirror a few days earlier. But tonight she had seen someone else, the face was not clear but she knew instantly that it was not Stacy making another appearance, there had been another girl murdered, she was sure of it. She thought about calling Captain Johnson, he had left her his card last week, he seemed nice enough but he was to interested in her past, her psychic ability, The last thing that Allison wanted was to be back in the news, ridiculed by her peers, accused of being a fraud, a fake. She didn't want to be hounded by the press, she didn't want to have to move again, she liked Bakersfield. But she had to talk to some one about this, the dead were reaching out to her, they wanted help and for some reason they wanted it from her. She put the Captains card back into her purse deciding not to call, she wanted to help these girls but she decided to be selfish a while longer, she crumpled up the newspaper and tossed it into the waste paper basket. "Two points." She hollered. Henry, the beagle pup she had brought home with her from the pet shop looked up at her. She hadn't felt like being alone and ever since the break in at the pet shop they had both been upset so she decided they needed each other, for the time being she had a new room mate named Henry. She shed her clothing leaving pieces scattered from the kitchen to the bathroom, she turned on the hot water, Henry stood at the door watching her intensely.

"I'll just be a few minutes Henry and then I will take you outside before bedtime. She promised, the puppy wagged his tail at her. She climbed into the shower and quickly washed her hair, she wanted to linger because it felt so good, she had spent all day cleaning cages and aquariums at work and she still felt like the snakes were slithering across her arms, one day she hoped to hire some one else to do that job, she figured there were probably several teen aged boys willing to play with snakes but right now she couldn't afford to hire any of them, it just was not in her budget, and there was no way her current helper Louisa was about to put her hand in a reptile cage. She could hear Henry begin to fuss a bit. She pulled the curtain back and reached for a towel. "What's wrong?" She asked Henry. He sat with his back to her looking out into the hallway. She wrapped the towel around her and stepped out into the hall. " Come on, let's go see what has your hair standing on end." Henry was reluctant to follow her but when she did finally coax him out of the bathroom he was right on her heels, the curtain in the living room was blowing as if the window were open but Allison knew she hadn't left a window open, the puppy began to bark and carry on and even pee'd in the floor leaving a nice little puddle on the carpet for her to clean up.

Allison double checked the window, it was shut and locked tight, when she turned around to reassure Henry that everything was all right she saw the newspaper article that she had crumpled up and threw away was now out of the can and laying in the floor, no longer crumpled up. The face of Stacy Peebles was staring up at her. "Why won't you just leave me alone? I can't help you." She picked up the paper ready to tear it into a million tiny pieces but something stopped her, instead she spread out the paper on the table and placed her hand flat on the girls face, flashes ran through her mind, she closed her eyes, she saw the dead girl, at first she was happy and smiling and then she turned angry, she was arguing with some one, Allison saw red but it was not blood she kept seeing the letter D flash in her mind and then as quickly as the visions came they had disappeared. Henry whined again looking up at her from the wet spot on the carpet.

"It's ok Henry I can clean that right up, I know you didn't mean to do it. That girl won't hurt you." She put a leash around Henry's neck and took him into the back yard, he really couldn't go anywhere because the yard was fenced but it was dark and she wanted to keep him close just in case. Henry quickly finished what he had started in the house, Allison looked around the yard, she saw nothing but she felt as if some one were watching her, she scooted the pup back into the house and locked the door behind her. She put the leash on the counter and quickly hopped into bed, she had made a pallet for Henry on the floor beside her bed but he was having none of that, he jumped onto the bed and dove under the covers all the way to the foot where he curled up around Allison's feet, they were both asleep in no time. Allison had been thankful that the next morning was Sunday, her only day off and that she could sleep in, that was if Henry would allow her to do so. However at eight thirty that morning there was a knock at the door.

"Who on earth would be here this early on a Sunday morning? " She asked Henry. But he wasn't budging. What few friends she did have knew better that to show up at that time of day. She decided it couldn't be anyone she knew she pulled the pillow back over her head to drown out the noise but who ever was at the door was not going to give up.

"Go away." She yelled in frustration.

"Police Mam. Open up." She sat up in bed. Why were the police at her door? Had something happened? Maybe her store had been broke into again. She jumped out of bed and grabbed a robe as she headed to the front door with Little Henry right behind her.

She swung the door open to see Captain Don Johnson standing there. "What's wrong? Did some one break into my shop again? Are the animals ok?"

"Calm down Miss Kramer, as far as I know your shop is fine." She bent down and picked up Henry, she turned from the doorway and Captain followed her inside shutting the door behind him. "I'll tell you Captain, I don't appreciate getting woke up this time of day on my only day off."

"It's almost nine Miss Kramer, I've already been up for four hours, and at least you get a day off, crime never takes a day off."

Allison had made her way into the kitchen poured Henry a bowl of dry food and rummaged around for the coffee filters, she stretched to reach them off the top shelf dropping one as she pulled them down, she picked it up off the floor and blew it off before sticking it into the pot. "Would you like some coffee Captain?"

"Yes I would, thank you!"

"Your lucky you're a man of the law or I would have booted you out by now and been back in bed fast asleep….actually I wouldn't have opened the door at all."

"Then I consider myself lucky." He took a seat on the sofa noticing the crumpled picture of Stacy Peebles on the coffee table in front of him. " Did you have a bad night." He asked her.

"Why would you think that?" She came back into the room and handed him a cup of coffee. that's when she saw what he'd been looking at, why hadn't she gotten rid of that last night? She asked herself. She sat down in a chair across from him, Henry having finished his breakfast had waddled back in and sat down in front of the captains feet. He reached down and pet his soft head. Henry lapped up the attention. "Are you my little buddy from the shop?" He asked.

"That's Henry, he just wasn't the same after the break in so I brought him home with me."

"He will be much happier here."

"I think so too, but let's get down to why you're here Captain."

He took a deep breath. "There was another murder last night."

"Damn." Was her only response.

"You knew that already didn't you?"

"How could I know that?" She snapped at him.

"You sensed it."

She stood up and paced the floor. " I don't know anything about your case Captain."

"I don't believe you, why is that picture of Stacy on your table?" She didn't answer him.

"Please Miss Kramer, we have two dead girls now, killed the same way and we have no clues and no idea where to start looking." She stayed silent for what seemed like forever and finally she spoke.

"She was here last night."

"Stacy?"

"Yes." This was usually the moment when a person would start calling her a liar and fake and walk out on her but Captain Johnson stayed where he was. " What did she want? Did she say anything?"

Allison looked up from her mug. "You believe me?"

"Should I not believe you?"

"Most people don't when I tell them that a dead person has been to see me."

"Well Miss Kramer, I am not most people, I don't know a lot about psychic abilities and I don't know a lot about you but I am willing to take my chances, I'd like you to come in and work with us on this case."

Allison nearly spit out her coffee through her nose. "You want me to work with you?"

"Actually you would be working with Detective Lottle, it's his case but he seems to be having trouble with it."

"Maybe you should put a different detective on it." She suggested.

"Lottle is the best I have Miss Kramer, but this case is making him an emotional wreck especially with this second girl dead, obviously by the same killer. Lottle likes to work alone but he's going to need help on this one."

"Then get him some help, another detective, I can't help you Captain."

"I think you can, you just don't want to."

She stood up again to pace the floor. "Your right, the last time I helped the police I got ran out of town, accused of being a fake and a fraud, I like it here and I don't want to have to move again. I'll tell you what I saw, a happy teenage girl one second and a dead one the next and the letter D, that letter kept coming up in my mind."

Captain Johnson was making notes in his little blue notepad.

"That's all I can tell you." She insisted.

"I didn't mean to upset you Miss Kramer, but it's clear that I have done just that. I am not asking for your help because I want to put you in the spot light I am asking for the sake of these girls and the others that might meet the same fate, we can keep you undercover bring you in as a new detective only you, I and Lottle will know the truth."

"I'll have to think about it Captain."

"Ok, fair enough, you think about it and I will keep bugging you until you say yes."

"Lets get one thing straight captain, no more banging on my door on a Sunday morning."

"Promise, my official hours to prod you will be Monday thru Friday between the hours of nine and five."

"Fine." She giggled. She couldn't help but like the man even if she didn't like what he was asking from her.

"The letter D huh?"

"Yes, you might want to have your detective Lottle check into that."

"I will, you still have my card right?"

"Yes I do."

"Good, I hope to be hearing from you soon."

"Don't count on it Captain, I'm really not interested in getting involved."

"My dear, your already involved, like it or not." He handed her his empty coffee mug.

"Thanks for the coffee."

"Anytime....except on Sunday." She added.

He bent down and scratched Henry's head once more on the way out, Henry loved it.

"Traitor." she hissed at the pup as she followed the Captain to the door."

"Good day Miss Kramer."

"It could have been had you not shown up."

"That's just your guilty conscience talking."

"I have nothing to feel guilty about."

"If you say so Miss Kramer." He put his sunglasses on, she watched as he made his way down the sidewalk to his car, he gave her a little wave as he pulled away.

She turned back to Henry. "What was that all about? He scratched your head and suddenly he's your best friend." Henry whined sensing that she was upset. "Great, now I'm taking it out on an innocent puppy. I know it's not your fault Henry, maybe I am just feeling a little guilty." Henry licked her hand.

Six

Jeremy rolled out of bed and crawled to the bathroom, he was worshiping the porcelain God this Sunday morning, of all things he had gotten food poisoning last night. He'd been craving Chinese from the Rice Hut but when he got there and heard there would be a thirty minute wait he decided to go else where, he'd waited all day to eat and he didn't want to wait any longer, he had found another Chinese place on Chester avenue that was virtually empty so he stopped there instead. Now he knew why the place had been empty. He would have to make a call to his buddy the health inspector, just as soon as he stopped vomiting, and his head stopped pounding. It was so not a good time for this he thought to himself, but really when was a good time for food poisoning. He had heard his phone ring at several different times earlier in the morning but he couldn't muster the energy to reach over and pick it up, finally he grabbed the cord and just unplugged it so he wouldn't have to hear it anymore. It could only have been bad news anyway.

He pulled himself up from the floor and washed his hands and face, he stumbled to the kitchen and fumbled with the aspirin bottle until it finally succumbed, he chewed a handful grabbed a bottled water and made his way back to bed. Then he heard his cell phone ring, he really wanted to ignore it but when that phone rang he knew it was business and he decided he had better answer it. "Hello." He whispered.

"Lottle." Came the booming voice of Captain Johnson. " Have you got a hangover? Why haven't you answered your phone?" Jeremy's head was pounding hard now. "Can you lower your voice please." He whispered into the phone.

"No, if you have a hangover you deserve what you get."

"For your information it's food poisoning."

"Got some bad Chinese did you?" Captain Joked.

"As a matter of fact I did."

"Funny, me and Phyllis ate at The Rice Hut last night and we are just fine."

"It wasn't the Rice Hut."

"You should have ate at The Rice Hut, anyway I'm a block from your place I'll be right there." Jeremy would have protested if he'd had the chance but the Captain had hung up already. He didn't feel like seeing anyone especially his loud mouth Captain. He rolled out of bed and walked to the door opening it just as captain was reaching for the Door bell. "I know you weren't going to ring that."

"I was, but you beat me to it." He looked Lottle up and down. "You could have put some pants on."

"What? If you don't like my boxers you can leave, I don't recall inviting you anyway."

He slouched down into his recliner, Captain sat across from him making himself entirely to comfortable as far as Jeremy was concerned. He picked things up and set them back down at least three times before Jeremy finally asked. " What is it? Why are you here on a Sunday?"

"I just came from seeing the pet shop owner."

"Oh yes, the old gypsy you told me about…oh I'm sorry I think you said she was smoking hot….or something like that."

"She is hot." Captain said.

"As hot as Phyllis?"

Captain turned red. After his date with her last night he now knew just how hot Phyllis could be. "You Don't even talk to me about Phyllis."

"Fine, why are you here?"

"The pet shop owner has some information that might help us on the case."

"What kind of information?"

"Here's the thing, and I don't want to hear any lip from you Lottle."

"Lip from me, come on Cap."

"Allison saw Stacy Peebles."

"What do you mean saw her?"

"As in saw her, she appeared to her and basically asked for her help to find her killer."

Jeremy held his head in his hands. "I can't believe your falling for this Cap, she's after attention good or bad, do you really believe a dead girl talked to her?"

"Miss Kramer is for real."

"How do you know that? How can you be so sure?"

"She worked on a case with the Los Angeles police and she helped them tremendously but the media did a number on her, she moved here to get away from it."

"It makes no sense why she would want to help with this case, if it could mean getting put in the same situation again."

"She doesn't really want to be involved with our case."

"Then why in the hell are we having this conversation?"

"She Can't control what she sees and who approaches her, she is clearly upset about knowing anything about this case."

"Please tell me you didn't ask her to work with us on this."

"I did."

"I hate it when you go behind my back on things like this Cap."

"I knew you would be against it."

"So you did it anyway. Why?"

"Simple, we have two dead girls and nothing to go on except the letter D, and that little tidbit of information came from Allison."

"Are you insinuating that I can't do my job? because I don't have a clue."

Captain laughed at him. "Lottle, you're the best damn detective that I've got and that I've ever had working for me, I've never seen you struggle so much as you have with this case and I know we have had some doozies."

Jeremy jumped up from his seat and ran to the bathroom again, his ribs ached from vomiting so much and he was simply amazed that he had anything left to throw up.

"Sorry again about your food poisoning Lottle."

"Oh this time it's the thought of working with your psychic making me sick."

He yelled from the doorway.

"You may have lost your cookies but at least you still have your sense of humor."

"Who said I was joking?"

"It doesn't matter anyway, I suggest you get used to the thought because as soon as she says yes you will be working with Miss. Kramer."

"Now your predicting she will say yes, are you a psychic too?"

"Just going with my gut on this one." He patted his belly.

Jeremy emerged from the bathroom having cleaned up from his latest attack. "Maybe your gut is just telling you to lay off the fast food Cap."

"Funny, one of these days Lottle, that quick wit is going to get you a black eye."

"You know I'm joking with you."

"Yes, but the next guy might not know that."

"I'll keep that in mind."

"Good, get some rest, see you bright and early in the morning."

"Well now, that depends on how late me and Phyllis stay out." He grinned.

"Don't even go there Lottle, that lady is off limits to you."

"Yes sir."

Bright and early Monday morning Jeremy sat at his desk looking over the photos of the two college girls, they looked so much alike they could have been related. There had to be a connection to them both being dead certainly no one just decided to wake up and go kill all the young blond haired blue eyed coeds they could find, at least he hoped no one thought that way, if so there would be a million unsuspecting potential victims walking the streets of Bakersfield.

Captain Johnson poked his head into Jeremy's office. "I see you made it, what's your game plan this morning?"

"I'm just prolonging the inevitable."

"What does that mean?"

"I'm going to the Drake residence this morning to speak to Jill's parents.

"I thought you would have spoken to them last night."

"I just couldn't bring myself to tell them so I sent a uniform." He hung his head down as if he had a reason to be ashamed of himself for not going in person.

"Who did you send?"

"Your new guy Sampson."

"I hope he was gentle."

"I'm sure he was, after all you seem to trust the kid."

"I don't know him enough to trust him, but so far he seems to be a pretty good beat cop—gotta go see a lady about a cup of coffee, good luck."

"Thanks." Jeremy knew that he wasn't going to get anywhere sitting at his desk so he finally got up and headed out the door to the Drake's home. He drove up Panama Lane until he found nineteen ten, he knocked on the door and a fragile looking boy answered, but what really got his attention was the girl standing a few feet behind him, he thought he had seen a ghost. The girl moved closer and put her hands on the boys shoulders As if to protect him from this stranger. "Can I help you?"

Jeremy pushed aside the shock of seeing the girl who had to be the sister of Jill because she was close enough to be her twin.

"I'm detective Lottle and I was wanting to speak to your parents if I may."

"You should have been here last night detective."

"I'm sorry."

"You had a better chance at getting your questions answered last night before the shock wore off, maybe if you had come instead of sending your flunky you would have learned something."

Jeremy's heart sank, he knew he should have come himself, he wondered if maybe Sampson had said something to offend the family was he cruel or heartless?

He wondered if he had made a mistake he could not fix. "I apologize if officer Sampson said or did anything out of line.

"He was fine, what I mean is that my parents were in shock last night it took a while to sink in that Jill is gone, they could have answered your questions last night but this morning is another story." The young boy darted out of the girls grip and ran down a long hallway. "What are you telling me?"

"My parents are so out of it that I don't know if they can talk at all, I went in to check on them this morning and I found some empty pill bottles, pain pills, I guess they took them to get to sleep…. They are ok, just out of it." She added.

He cocked his head and looked at her. "Your concern is written on your face."

"Would you mind if I come in and look around maybe I can get some answers that way."

"I don't know how that would help you but come in, knock yourself out." She moved aside so that he could enter the house. He stepped into the spacious living room, the first thing he saw was a massive television set, it must have been seventy inches or more, for a moment all he thought about was how cool it would be to watch his weekly NASCAR racing on that screen, it would be almost as good as being there in person. He heard a noise coming from the corner of the room bringing him out of his daydream. The girl was pulling pictures from a shelf and putting them into boxes that she had stacked on a kitchen table. "Excuse me, I didn't catch your name."

"That's because I didn't throw it at you." She continued what she was doing with out looking up at him.

"Ok, I just thought that it might be easier if I addressed you by name, so you'd know when I'm talking to you."

"I'm the only one in the room detective I think I'll know if your talking it must be to me…but if you insist on knowing my name it's Janet."

"That's a pretty name for a pretty girl."

"Spare me the niceties detective."

"Ok." He walked closer to her, she wasn't out to make a new friend that much was true. Jeremy saw something in one of the pictures that looked familiar, he took the photo right out of her hand and studied it. There were several blonde headed girls all dressed in cheerleading uniforms, the same uniforms he'd seen at Stacy's funeral.

"So you like cheerleaders do you?" She asked him.

"Some of them look familiar, like the girls at Stacy's funeral."

"I don't doubt they were all there and they were probably wearing their pretty little uniforms."

"Yes. I thought that was odd."

"For them it's normal behavior detective, to this group of girls cheerleading is everything."

"And your not one of them?"

"No, I have better things to do with my time. But academics have never been first in this family cheerleading has always been more important." She sounded bitter.

"Are you talking about your sister?"

"No, I am talking about my parents, my accomplishments have meant nothing to them, president of the debate team all the scholarships I've already gotten, Jill and her cheerleading have always been more important to them."

"Who the hell are you?" A slurred female voice asked from behind them. He turned to see Janet's mother standing in the doorway trying to get her eyes to focus on him.

"I'm detective Lottle."

"Little?"

"Lottle."

"Whatever, what do you want?"

"I wanted to ask you a few questions."

"Unless you're here to tell me Jill is not dead I have nothing to say to you."

She walked toward the table where Janet stood, nearly falling on her face. "Can't wait to get rid of your sister huh? You're a selfish little shit." She grabbed Janet by the shirt collar "How dare you try to get rid of these pictures."

"I just thought it would make things easier for you mom."

"You want to know what would make it easier for me? If you had died instead of your sister, it wouldn't surprise me if you killed her." She shook Janet hard by the arm before slumping to the floor in a fit of tears. Jeremy pulled Janet closer to him he thought surely it was only the mothers grief speaking but still he thought what a harsh thing for Janet to have to hear from her own mother.

"You may look just like your sister but you will never be her." Mrs. Drake pulled herself up off the floor and flopped down into a chair, she pulled a tiny bottle of whiskey out of her pocket and drank it in one swallow.

"I should go." He told Janet. " Is there any where else I could take you?" He asked thinking that maybe she would not want to stay in the house and continue to be treated like dirt.

"No, I should be here just in case they need me."

"You're a better person than I would be in this situation. Call me if you need me, or if there is anything you can think of that would help me figure out who would want to murder your sister."

"I will detective and you can take that picture if you think it might help you in any way."

"Thanks." He had to force his feet to move, he was sad for Janet, she was just a child herself and she didn't deserve to be treated like she was not wanted by her own mother, sometimes he just could not figure people out.

Seven

The McFarland High cheerleaders stood lined up, waiting for their newly appointed head cheerleader to show, apparently she had called an unscheduled meeting for reasons none of them could figure out. Stacy Peebles had been head cheerleader the previous year and as head of the squad she had the power to choose her predecessor and after careful consideration she had chosen Destiny Gamble. Destiny had been the one who wanted it most and she had been willing to do almost anything to get to the top and now she was there.

"All right you lazy, good for nothing people. I have a surprise for you." Destiny walked up and down in front of the girls acting like a drill sergeant. "We are going to attempt the three tier pyramid."

The girls looked at one another. " But Destiny, that is to dangerous."

"Shut your trap Ronda, I'm the head of this squad, and I will tell you what we are going to do—is that clear?"

The girls were confused, something had gotten into Destiny and they didn't like it. She passed out orders of who was to be where in the pyramid. "And Lisa, you get to be on top."

"I'm afraid of heights, you know that."

"Get over it—fear nothing. You are the lightest and you will be on top."

Lisa was not happy with this, not happy at all, and neither were the other girls. Instead of arguing they decided to try it Destiny's way, they constructed the pyramid just as Destiny had ordered and now it was Lisa's turn.

"You can do it." Encouraged Holly."

"I'm scared."

"But you can do this Lisa we all know you can."

Lisa began to climb to the third tier as the others offered words of encouragement.

"I did it, I made it." She boasted with pride. But she got over confident with her achievement because she began to topple and soon she was tumbling to the ground taking the others with her. Lisa landed on the ground with a thud and loud snap that was obviously a bone breaking. "I think my leg is broke." She screamed in pain.

The girls scrambled to get up so they could tend to her. Destiny watched with an evil grin on her face.

"See if you can put some weight on it."

Lisa struggled but there was no way she was going to be able to walk by herself, her right leg was in excruciating pain.

"I can't I need help."

"This is all your fault Destiny."

"Listen Holly, you can't blame me for your stupidity or Lisa's. Your all incompetent, I should have you all replaced."

"We should have you replaced."

"Go ahead and try it." She smiled at Holly.

"We will." The entire squad turned their backs on Destiny and helped Lisa get to the nurses office where Nurse Noble confirmed there was definitely a break in Lisa's right leg, she called her parents to come get her, Lisa's parents joined the girls in the principals office to demand that Destiny be removed from the squad and suspended from school for no less than ten days. Principal Marsha Kinney agreed.

The next day The Cheer squad And principal Kinney greeted Destiny with cold stares.

"What's going on?"

"As if you don't know."

"No, Holly. I don't know, that's why I asked."

Principal Kinny stepped forward. "Miss Gamble from this moment on you are no longer a member of this cheer squad and you are also suspended form school for the next ten days because of your recent behavior.

"I don't understand. What did I do?"

"Please do not waste any of our time with your silly questions, you are fully aware of why you are being punished and there is nothing you can say to change my mind."

"But Miss Kinney……

Principal Kinney held her hand up. " I don't want to hear any excuses destiny, you can go home now." She turned and walked away.

"I don't understand." She said to the girls. Her gaze rested on Lisa's leg cast. "Are you all right?" She asked her.

Lisa adjusted her crutches before she spoke. "It's a little late for your concern and no, I'm not all right my leg is broken and I will be in this cast for six weeks…thanks to you."

"Me, I didn't break your leg."

"Shut up Destiny, what's done is done."

"I still don't understand." She wanted an explanation, she wanted to know why all of a sudden they had all turned against her, after all that she had done for them. They had all been happy for her when Stacy had announced that she would be taking over as her predecessor and now they have booted her off the squad with out the slightest explanation, it wasn't fair. She wanted to cry, but she wasn't about to let them see her do it. When she was feeling lonely and down like she was right then, there was only one person who could make her feel better.

*

Two Years Earlier

The Gamble family drove along interstate five on their way to Klamath Falls Oregon, they went there every year for vacation. Tom and Vanessa, and their blonde haired blue eyed triplets who sat in the back seat, Destiny, Dalana, and Dustin, they were bickering as usual.

"I thought triplets were supposed to be close, read each others minds, feel each others pain and all that crap." Said Tom, who was clearly frustrated with his children's bad behavior. He looked in the rear view mirror at his teenagers.

"I think that just works with twins dear." Vanessa chimed in.

"So with triplets they just argue and hate each other. Is that what your telling me?"

"I'm not telling you anything dear, except maybe that they are teenagers, cut them some slack."

"I'll cut them some slack when they give me a break."

"I'm sorry Daddy." Destiny said in a sweet voice.

"Suck up." Dalana said.

"Leave your sister alone Dalana, at least she has the good manners to apologize, you should follow her lead."

"Tom." Vanessa gave him a stern look. She had been trying to get Tom to be nicer towards Dalana for a long time, he seemed to single her out, there was no other way to put it, he was plain mean to her and she noticed it. That's why she was so jealous of her siblings.

"Why do you hate me so much Daddy? What have I done to make you hate me so much?" Dalana asked.

Destiny jabbed her elbow into Dalana's right side trying to get her to shut up, Dustin did the same from her left side. Dustin began to shake uncontrollably. Dalana looked at him, he was weak, she thought. Dustin had always been weak and paranoid, if he'd had a tail it would have always been between his legs. Dalana looked at him, it was like looking in a mirror. Almost, aside from her and Destiny he had short blonde hair and the slightest dimple in his chin, he did look like a weak little girl, except for he had a penis. At least she assumed he did. Now, she and Destiny were identical, in looks at least, but when Destiny opened her mouth the difference was clear, she was an ass kisser, she could be drippy sweet to get her way but when she didn't she was a total bitch, especially to Dalana, she might have had their dad fooled but Dalana was onto her. She was always hugging and kissing on him, Dalana wondered what dad would think if he knew that Destiny was sneaking over to the neighbors house after everyone was asleep. That guy was like fifteen years older than her. It would serve her right if she spilled the beans about that right here in the car. Dalana looked straight ahead catching her fathers eyes in the mirror. He had a cold stare focused right on her.

"Look out." Vanessa yelled.

Tom swerved trying to avoid the oncoming truck headed straight for them. Tires screeched and metal crunched and they ended up on the wrong side of the road, Tom heard horns honking, he smelled smoke, flames were licking out from under the car, Vanessa was breathing but she was unconscious Tom pulled her from the car and safely off the road. He went back for Destiny and lifted her from the car, he could see that Dalana was struggling with her seatbelt, unable to break free of it. Dustin had some how been ejected from the car and lay off to the side of the road, Tom could see him stirring, he was alive.

"Daddy, help me." Dalana pleaded from her seat in the car, the flames obscured her view of him slightly, the fire was getting worse. She struggled to get loose but the belt was not budging. Vanessa came to just as he was reaching her with Destiny and Dustin had managed to crawl to them. Vanessa looked at him and the children. " Dalana." She asked.

Tom couldn't look his wife in the eye. At that moment the car exploded, fully engulfed in flames now. Vanessa screamed forcing herself to get up off the pavement, she ran towards the car but a second explosion stopped her. Tom had waited to long, now there was no chance of saving his other daughter, there was no way she could have escaped that car before it burst into flames. Vanessa looked at her husband knowing full well that he hadn't tried to save Dalana, he hadn't wanted to save her. In sixteen years she never doubted her love for him but now she had to wonder what kind of monster had she married.

Dalana's memorial was just that, there was no body to mourn over all they had were the memories of her, some of them good, most of them bad. Vanessa Gamble and her son stood side by side in front of a large picture of Dalana it was her sixteenth birthday picture taken only days before the fatal crash, she stared back at them but there was something about the look in her eyes that scared Dustin, Dalana had scared him, long before now.........

*

Denstiny scrambled to get away from school, away from the people who had so boldly betrayed her. She walked quickly three blocks west, her heart raced until she saw the familiar building of Rustling winds, the sanitarium that her mother and her brother both called home now. She breezed through the front door.

"Hello Destiny." Nurse Sonny called out. She usually stopped at the front desk to talk to the nurse but today she just wanted to see her brother, he always had a way of calming her nerves. She waved quickly at the nurse and headed down the east corridor her anxiety eased a bit once she entered the room and saw her brothers blond hair peeking out from the blankets.

"Hey lazy boy, why are you still in bed?" She walked closer to him, he pulled the blankets all the way up over his head. " Dustin, what's wrong?" She put her hand on his shoulder but he shrugged her off.

"He had a rough night." Nurse Sonny was standing in the doorway.

"What do mean? What happened?"

"The night shift reports that something spooked him, he insists that some one was in his room after hours."

"Who?"

"He said it was you."

"But I wasn't here, and even if I were why would he be scared of me?"

"I don't know, I'm just telling you what I was told."

Destiny tried to coax her brother out from under the blanket. "Dustin honey, come out and talk to me." She pleaded. He refused becoming more agitated with her.

"Maybe you should just give him some time alone."

"No Sonny, I have to know what happened and who scared him. I'm all he's got Mom has completely lost her senses and Dad is to busy with all his younger women to bother visiting him."

"I know Destiny, but maybe it would be better to give him time."

Dustin peeked out from the blankets to look at her, he watched as a single tear escaped from her eye. "Desty." He sat up in bed and reached for her. She hugged him. He didn't say much anymore, his sentences were broken but she usually figured out what he was trying to tell her. He pushed her away but he was still smiling at her. "You scared me Dustin."

"Desty scare me too." She looked to nurse Sonny but she was of no help, she shrugged her shoulders and left the room.

"How did I scare you Dustin?"

"Desty under bed."

"I was never under your bed Dustin." He got restless again. "Yes Desty under bed."

"No." She argued until he grew tired and gave up on her. "Walk." She helped him out of his bed and they walked down the hall to the dinning room, the usually went to the garden but it was raining outside so they went into the dinning hall where they found their mother sitting all alone in front of the television, she had that usual blank stare, not acknowledging that they were there. The staff started bringing in dinner trays.

"I better get going Dustin."

"No stay with me."

"You have to eat dinner, take your bath and then go to bed."

"Don't wanna sleep."

"You need your sleep Dustin, no crazy antics tonight ok. Give the night shift a break."

"Ok Desty, ok."

"I love you Dustin."

"I love Desty." She kissed him on the cheek and left, stopping at the desk on her way out she asked the nurses to call her if anything out of the ordinary happened that night. It had been one confusing day and now all she wanted to do was go home and take a long hot bubble bath.

Eight

Jeremy sat in front of his twenty seven inch television set and watched the ball drop in times square. He was alone again on this new years eve, with no one to kiss and no one to keep him company except the photos of the dead teenage girls, he was still beating himself up over the deaths of Stacy and Jill, still all he had to go on was the letter D, given to him by Allison Kramer. Maybe he should give the lady a chance, maybe he should just swallow his pride and ask for her help maybe... Damn phone, it never stopped ringing, he snatched it up. "What" He spat into the receiver.

"Detective, this is dispatch. Captain Johnson would like you to meet him over at the Bakersfield campus."

"Doreen, Please tell me it isn't at the girls dorm."

"No Sir, actually it's on the football field, fifty yard line."

"Shit. Sorry Doreen. Please tell him I'll be right there."

"Will do, detective." He was almost positive that he was going to get there and find a blonde haired girl spread out on the green field, strangled like the others. But what he saw when he arrived was a young man, he had been stabbed in the chest. There were two girls standing by the bleachers they looked upset. "Witnesses." Captain Johnson said pointing to them. Obviously they hadn't been questioned yet. "We saved them for you."

"As if I don't have enough on my plate already… Have you got an ID on the boy yet?"

"Nothing on him." At least he wouldn't have to tell his family tonight.

Jeremy questioned the girls but they were of little help, they denied ever seeing the boy before, he let them go home and took the Polaroid picture of the kid out of a CSI's hand.

"Hey, give that back."

"Sorry, take another picture chuck, this one is going home with me."

"Fine." Chuck was about as happy to be there as he was but then again chuck wasn't the easiest person to get along with, he was crabby a lot.

Jeremy trudged up to the school office to see if he could get his hands on a year book, maybe he could ID this kid from that.

"No sir you can not take this book off the premises."

"Come on lady, this is a police investigation."

"No." She said again, This lady and Chuck would make a good couple he thought.

He decided to try a different approach, he looked directly into her eyes and batted his eyelashes. "Pleeeease. I promise I'll return it in the morning."

She hesitated for a brief moment. "Ok." She pushed the book back across the counter towards him. "But I want it back tomorrow."

"I promise." Holy cow, it worked. He knew a woman could get her way by batting her eyelashes but he didn't think it would ever work for him.

He tucked the book under his arm and winked at her as he left. At least he could go home and rest for a little while being that he didn't have to inform the family yet, first he had to find the family. And to do that he had to figure out who the dead boy was.

As he drove home it started to rain. "I love a rainy night, I love a rainy night…. He sang with Eddie Rabbit on the radio, they played that song every time it rained. He would never sing in front of any one but since he was alone he belted it out not caring. He pulled up into his driveway and sat in the car, the engine still running the wiper blades still swooshing side to side, he noticed his garage needed painting, the whole house needed painting really, maybe if he cleaned his garage out he could actually park in it and he wouldn't have to worry about getting soaked running from the driveway to the front door when it was raining. He shrugged. Maybe some day he would actually have some free time to fix things up around the place, maybe one day he would actually take a vacation. Maybe it would lift his spirits, pull him out of his funk so to speak. He grabbed the yearbook and made a mad dash for the front door, rain pelted him hard on the head and shoulders. "Ouch." He fumbled with his keys, upon entering the house the phone was ringing again. "Yep." He answered.

"Lottle, we have an ID on the dead kid." Silence took over.

"Well, don't keep me in suspense Cap."

"We got him to the morgue and did a run on his prints." Sally says he has a record.

"Really."

"Long as my arm. Breaking and entering, auto theft, drug activity, assault with a deadly weapon. Four counts of attempted rape."

"Four?"

"Yep all different women and guess who the fourth one was?"

"Who?"

"Jill drake."

"Really?"

"Yep, and by the way kid's name was Jim Gunner, no family so to speak."

"Jim Gunner, doesn't sound like a criminal name."

"No, but he was on his way to a long term prison sentence."

"Some one took it into their own hands and gave him the death sentence."

"Funny Lottle."

"It wasn't meant to be funny."

"Oh, well, goodnight then."

"Night." No sooner had he hung the phone up it started to ring again, he was surprised to hear the voice of Janice Deets on the other end of the line.

"What can I do for you Janice?"

"I was going through some papers tonight and I found a notebook that belonged to Jill, I guess she must have left it one of the times we studied together…. Jeremy flipped through the college yearbook while he waited for Janice to get to her point, he was looking through last years year book so Stacey and Jill's pictures would not be in this one. "I found some e mails printed out that I thought might interest you, they are from a Tom Wall to Stacey, it seems that they might have been interested in the same guy…maybe that's why they stopped speaking to each other."

"Do me a favor Janice, put those in a safe place and tell no one about them."

"I can do that, would you like me to bring them to you now?"

"No, it's very late I think they can wait until the morning."

"I can bring them to your house in the morning."

"I don't think it would be a good idea for you to come to my house."

"I can bring them to your work."

"That will be fine, say about nine thirty."

"I'll see you then."

"Thanks Janice."

"I'll do anything for you detective Lottle." She quickly hung up.

Was there some hidden meaning in that sentence? She was trying awfully hard to let him agree to come to his house. It was late and he was surly reading more into that than really was. He sat on his broke down couch and continued to look through the book, in the senior pictures he found a Tom Wall. "What the hell would they see in this guy?"

Tom wall did not look like the kind of guy that beautiful cheerleaders would be interested in, he was overweight and still had acne at the time that picture was taken, Jeremy could hardly stand to look at the poor kid. He slammed the book shut and turned on the television, re runs of different strokes. "What you talkin bout Willis?" He mimicked the younger brother on the show. Oh lord Jeremy, you need a woman. He told himself, right before he dozed off.

*

Allison lay in bed looking up at the ceiling, listening to the rain beat down on the roof. Usually the rain helped her sleep but not tonight, it was new years eve, actually now it was the early hours of new years day, something was nagging at her but she couldn't put her finger on it, she slid out of bed and waddled lazily to the refrigerator pulling out a piece of chocolate cake and what was left of a quart of milk. Henry, as usual was at her feet looking up at her. "I know, I know, I shouldn't be eating this late at night, early in the morning. Whatever."

"Ruff."

She looked down at him again. "I'm fully aware that this will go straight to my thighs."

"Ruff" He said again.

"Your definitely a male Henry." She reached into the cub bard and pulled out a doggy bone. Henry took it carefully out of her hand and ran back to the bedroom. "Just like a man, take what you want and get the heck out of here." She yelled after him.

Allison sat on the floor in front of the television, propped up against the couch she scanned the channels stopping on different strokes, she hadn't seen that show in years, she laughed between bites of cake and gulps of milk. The little kid was a hoot, maybe it was funny because it was so late at night who knew but for some reason she watched the entire episode before falling asleep on the living room floor, she dreamed strange dreams, that usually happened when she ate late at night or early in the morning, but she kept dreaming of a cougar and it was attacking her, but yet it wasn't her, it was as if she were in some one else's body. And the letter D kept floating through her mind.

When Allison awoke it wasn't from the dreams but from Henry licking her face, She sat up and rubbed the sleep from her eyes. "Hey buddy." He rolled over so that she could rub his belly, as she rubbed she continued to see flashes of the cougar from her dreams an angry cougar with sharp teeth and a thirst for blood, she stopped rubbing Henry's belly, he nudged at her hand trying to get her to continue. " Sorry buddy, I think I need to make a phone call real quick." She jumped up off the floor and ran to her purse, she fished through the junk until she found Captain Johnsons business card. I guess it's time to put this to use. She told herself.

"I'm so glad you called Ms. Kramer."

"I thought I might have some useful information for you."

"Yes, but I know we could make better use of your information if you were working here at the station with detective Lottle."

"Captain, we have been through this already, I wouldn't be

comfortable working there, but I will tell you what I have over the phone."

"Well, let me here it."

"All last night I kept having dreams, visions of a cougar attacking me, or some one that looked like me, I thought maybe it was just the chocolate cake that I had eaten so late making me have weird dreams but the letter D was there again and I figured it must all be connected some how…does a cougar mean anything to you?"

"No, but I will be sure to mention it to Lottle, unless you want to tell him about it yourself."

"I'd rather not."

"Are you sure?" There was a long silence.

"I'm sure, at least for now."

"I don't know if I believe you Ms. Kramer."

"All right captain, this is bothering me more than I want to admit."

"Guilty conscience."

"I have nothing to feel guilty about Captain."

"If you have the ability to help us catch a killer and you don't then you will have something to feel guilty about."

"Gee thanks Captain, I feel so much better about things after that comment, your not helping any."

"Is my tactic working?"

Another long bout of silence before she finally spoke. "Ok Captain, you win. I'll be at your office in the morning, is that soon enough for you?"

"That will do, considering today is new years day."

"I'm not making you any promises Captain."

"Too late, you just said you would be there."

"Yes, but I meant I can't make any promises that I can help on this case, I'll do my best."

"I'm sure with you and my best detective working together that you can figure out who is responsible for these killings."

"I hope so Captain, I hope so."

Captain Johnson was elated, he had gotten the psychic to agree to work on the case, he hoped Lottle would warm up to the idea but he wouldn't bet any money on it. He called Jeremy and was almost happy when the voice mail picked up, he left him a brief message and quickly hung up.

Nine

Allison sat in her car out side of the police station located on the north end of Bakersfield, the engine still running. She still was not sure if she wanted to do this, actually she was sure that she didn't want to be there but she had already promised Captain Johnson that she would help out and she never backed out on a promise. Even though she kept thinking about the last time she helped the police, the circus that it had become, she did not want that kind of attention again. She wanted this killer to be found she honestly did but she did not know why they so desperately needed her to help find him. She did know the answer to that, the police didn't need her, the dead girls needed her, it was after all Stacey Peebles who came to her after her death. She haunted her more that she cared to admit. And that was the biggest reason that she had agreed to work with this detective Lottle character.

Allison heard a noise and looked into her side mirror, there was a man walking toward her car, she suddenly became nervous, he didn't look like an axe murderer or anything, actually he was a nice looking man but for some reason she felt intimidated by his presence. Surely he would not try to do anything to her right in front of the police station, that would be pretty bold, not to mention stupid. He was now only inches away from her door when he bent down and lifted up a pant leg, he adjusted a small hand gun in his ankle holster. Oh Lord! Was he going to shoot her? Was he going to go postal on some one in the station? Should she call and warn them? The man pulled down his pant leg and when he stood up she saw the badge he wore on his belt. She let out a sigh of relief. He was a cop, and not a bad looking one at that. Stop it. She told herself, your not looking for romance you're here to find a killer, if you ever get out of the car.

Tap tap. Allison jumped at the sound on her window, she turned to see captain Johnson grinning down at her. She slowly rolled the window down. "Your not thinking about backing out on me are you?"

"The thought did cross my mind Sir." She admitted.

"I hope that silly thought is out of your head, because now that you're here I'm not going to let you back out."

"Does your detective know that I'm coming?"

"I left him a voice mail last night."

"So you didn't talk to him in person?"

"He called me back." He was purposely being illusive.

"What did he say? I'm sure he was less than thrilled at the thought."

"I believe he said, I can't believe your bringing in some crystal ball toting, tarot card reading old hag in on this case. Or something of that nature." He gestured with his hands.

She looked straight ahead and rolled the window back up, she still had a grip on the steering wheel, her knuckles were white because of it.

"Please Ms. Kramer, Lottle will warm up to you I'm sure of it, just give him a chance."

She shook her head no. "I'm not asking for Lottle and I'm not asking for myself. I'm asking for those dead girls and their families I'm asking so that you might help us find this mad man before he takes any more lives."

"There are always going to be killers in the world Captain, we can't stop them all."

"I understand that Allison, but if we can just stop one killer we might save a dozen from being killed by him. Oh why did he have to say that? Now she felt guiltier than she had before, of course that's why he made the speech, he knew what it would do to her. "Oh, all right Johnson, you win." She turned off the engine and yanked the keys out of the ignition. He opened the door helping her out.

"Thanks."

"Your welcome." He grinned at her. She followed him up the side walk and through the front door of the station, there were several small offices to each side of the main room, he led her to one of those offices and shut the door behind them. "Have a seat, would you like some coffee?"

"Yes, please." He crossed the short space to where a coffee pot sat and he poured her a cup, she took the mug from him. Taking a sip from his own mug " Ahhhhh! that's some good stuff." He looked out the window into the larger main room and seemed to fixate on a slightly older but very pretty woman, the woman seemed to sense him and she looked His way and smiled back.

"I don't know what I would do with out my coffee making Phyllis."

"Is that all she's good for?"

"No, she's good for a lot of things, she's good for me."

Allison took a sip of coffee from her own number one cop mug. Phyllis did make a good cup of java.

"There's Lottle, hey Lottle, get in here." He yelled out the door.

Allison sat straight up in her chair, there were so many people milling about out there that she couldn't tell which guy he was talking to. None of them seemed to be coming their way.

"Lottle." Captain yelled in a louder, firmer voice. This time one of the men responded, not just any man, it was the good looking one that she had seen outside in the parking lot. The tall, thin man looked at captain Johnson with an angry expression, he knew he was about to meet the psychic and he was not happy about it.

Jeremy walked slowly towards the office, she watched his every movement, he was tall, she guessed about six foot two, short brown hair, olive colored skin, she couldn't see his eyes close enough but she was sure that whatever color they were they would be beautiful just like the rest of him. He entered, shut the door behind him and poured himself a cup of coffee, he sat down across from her and waited for some one to tell him why he was there.

"This is Allison Kramer, the psychic I told you about." Jeremy nearly spit out his coffee. He knew that Captain said she was good looking but he never believed it, he really expected to see an old gypsy lady.

"Not what you expected?" She asked him.

"No." He checked her out, even though she was sitting down he could tell she was around five foot seven, perfect, she had long blond hair and sparkling blue eyes, she was a hottie just like Cap had said she was, but what he didn't like was how much she looked like the two dead woman, a chill ran up his spine.

"I really don't know why you're here Ms. Kramer, to be totally honest I don't believe in psychics."

"So I hear Mr. Lottle, even so it's a pleasure to meet you." She held her hand out and he took it, giving it a firm shake. He noticed a faint smell of lilac. Sweet! He thought. Dropping her hand quickly. "I don't doubt that you're a nice person Ms. Kramer but I just don't think our working together is going to produce any leads that I can't come up with on my own." He glared at captain Johnson.

"Lottle, we have been over this a dozen times, Allison is here to help and you will give her every opportunity to do so. That is an order."

"Yes Sir." He stood and gave Johnson a soldiers salute on his way to the door. "Well, are you coming Ms. Kramer?"

"Oh, yes. I'm coming." She set the mug on the edge of the desk and grabbed her bag, this time his long legs carried him quickly and she had to jog to keep up, they made their way from the first office to the very last little office, he opened the door and motioned for her to go in, he checked her out, she was thin but curvy in all the right places just enough to hold onto, he thought. She was wearing a tank top with a light sweater over it, she had on loose fitting jeans and why on earth she was wearing those big ol boots he didn't know, they looked like hiking boots.

She sat down in an overstuffed chair and tried to make herself comfortable, as much as she could anyway considering the fact that Lottle was checking her out.

"Nice boots."

"Thanks." She crossed her legs. "Nice chair."

"Thanks." He shuffled some paperwork around on his desk. "A ha!" He pulled a particular folder out from a stack and opened it up in front of her, she leaned in to get a closer look. There were two different girls, they were obviously dead, they looked a lot alike.

"I just don't understand why some one would want to kill these girls."

"If I had all the answers you wouldn't be here." The aggravation clear in his voice.

"No, I guess not. But I think I can help you, captain Johnson thinks I can help you."

"What makes you so sure you can help?"

"Didn't Captain tell you ?"

"Tell me what? He stopped shuffling through papers to look at her.

"I've seen the girl in this picture." She pointed to the first girl, Stacey Peebles.

"When and where?"

"A few weeks ago, in my house."

"Why was she in your house?"

"She wants me to help find her killer."

"Your telling me she was in your house after she was dead? How is that even possible?"

"I really don't want to go into all of this right now."

"All of what? If your going to be working with me don't you think I should know what you see, because your telling me that you see dead people, and now you just want to leave it at that."

"I woke up one night having some bad dreams, I went to wash my face and when I looked up in the mirror I saw Stacy Peebles instead of my own reflection."

"Really?" He wasn't impressed.

"Did she say anything to you."

"No, I turned around thinking she was real and I would see her again but she disappeared."

"Was she already dead when this happened?"

"I think so, I heard about her murder on the news the next night."

"I don't understand why she would come to you."

"She thinks I can help you find her killer."

"Can you?"

"I will do what I can Mr. Lottle, that's why I'm here."

"Thought you were here because Cap asked you."

"Yes, he was very persuasive but Stacy is the real reason I'm here."

"I won't lie to you Ms. Kramer, I am not entirely convinced about your so called psychic abilities."

"I am used to it, there are a lot of skeptics in the world."

"Ok, I'll just say this Ms Kramer—"

"Please, call me Allison." She insisted.

"Fine, Allison. I will agree to give you two weeks on this case, if we don't get anywhere then you go your way and I will continue to work it on my own."

"Agreed, Jeremy, you have a deal, two weeks. Thank you for giving me a chance to help you."

"Don't thank me yet, just prove to me that I haven't made a mistake bringing you in."

Allison circulated through the crime scene photos, the girls were so young and pretty, why were they dead? Had they wronged someone? Were the deaths connected or was it a coincidence that they looked a lot alike and attended the same college.

"What are you thinking?" He asked her.

"I was wondering if the deaths were connected just because they look alike but now I See that they both had on the same underwear. That has to mean something."

"Christmas time, they were keeping with the spirit. I already noticed the red underwear."

"I wasn't implying that you had missed it, however did you notice that it is exactly the same?"

"What do you mean?" He stood over her shoulder and looked closer at the photos.

"It's hard to tell what kind of material it's made of in the photos but you can't miss how the bras are made they are underwire and a tiny red rose bud in the middle, and the panties, they have a slight design of some sort on them." She traced her finger over the picture. Upon closer investigation Jeremy could see that she was right, the red was obvious but all the other similarities he hadn't noticed and that just made him mad at himself, not at her, however he wanted to be mad at her, it was still eating at him that she was even there in the first place. "Are you sure you're a psychic and not a detective?"

"I have not had the official training that you have had but I do pay attention to detail and I'm sure that this lingerie was expensive. I'd like to see it in person."

"Let's go to the basement." He suggested.

"What's in the basement?" She asked nervously.

"The evidence room." He laughed.

"Of course, I knew that. I mean really why else would you be taking me down to the basement." She laughed at herself, feeling silly.

"The only other reason I can think of would be to make out with you in private."

"What?" She stopped laughing, as he ushered her through the open elevator door. she stopped abruptly causing him to crash into the back of her, he grabbed her at the waist to steady himself and her, he eased her the rest of the way into the elevator and turned her around to face him. Her face was red with embarrassment.

"Do you want to make out with me Allison?"

"I just met you, why would you even ask such a question?"

"Loosen up, will you." He told her. "I was just joking with you, can't you take a joke?"

"Of course I can, I just don't know how to read you yet."

"That's funny coming from a psychic." That should have miffed her off but she hadn't heard the comment, she was still thinking about making out with him, why would she want to? Just because the man was tall and handsome and smelled of old spice and his light brown eyes sparkled at her and his lips…. Why the heck was she looking at his lips? Why on earth was she so attracted to this man after just meeting him? None of those questions mattered anyway because he was just kidding, he didn't want to make out with her, she was ninety nine percent sure that he didn't even want her around. She could usually read people better than this, but she was off her game today.

"What if I had said yes?"

"Excuse me."

"What if I had said yes, I want to make out with you."

"Well then I would just have to grant you that wish." He leaned into her as if he just might kiss her but the elevator door chose that time to open and he pulled back. Two Female officers were waiting to get in, they looked at Allison and Jeremy and then back at each other, like they knew something that she didn't. Maybe he really did take women to the basement to make out with them. She was furious with herself for letting him fluster her like that.

"Turn right at the end of the hall." He barked at her.

"Yes master." She mumbled.

After fifteen minutes of searching the room they finally found the evidence they were looking for, Jeremy handed her some rubber gloves and told her to put them on.

"Always use these before touching evidence."

"I'm not stupid detective Lottle."

"I never thought that you were, I thought we had graduated to first names what happened?"

"The incident in the elevator happened, you made me feel like a fool."

"Why?"

"Can we just forget about it and move on to the evidence already?"

"First I'd like to know how I made you feel like a fool."

"Please Jeremy, let it go." He shrugged his wide shoulders and grabbed the box from the shelf, he lifted out a plastic bag containing the red bra and panties of Stacy Peebles.

"These were on Stacy when she was found." He carefully spread out the clothing for her to look at before pulling out the identical pair that Jill Drake had been wearing at the time of her death.

"Velvet." She said.

"Velvet, I see the design now. I just assumed maybe they were wearing red because of it being Christmas time."

"I think there is more to it than that."

He slammed his fist on the table making its contents shake.

"What was that for?"

"I can't believe I didn't see all of this before."

"Were the women sexually assaulted?"

"No evidence of sexual assault or of a redressing."

"Maybe they just had a heck of a sale at J.C. Penny's and that's all it amounts too." She giggled trying to lighten the mood in the room.

"Funny, What do you know, the psychic has a sense of humor."

"Thanks, and for your information I do not have a crystal ball."

"I didn't really think that you did."

She felt guilty for standing there joking when these girls were dead, they would never laugh again. "I know this is serious business Jeremy, I'm going to go home and see what I can figure out about all of this. Can I take the pictures with me?"

"I don't think that—"

"Please, I won't loose them, and I think maybe they will help me."

It was against his better judgment to let her take them because they were part of the evidence but he found it hard to say no to her.

*

Allison studied the photos of the dead girls over and over but nothing seemed to be clicking, she was getting nothing from them, no vibes no visions. It was very frustrating, usually she got a hint of a clue but this case was puzzling her as well, something was interfering with her abilities, her gift or her curse. She looked at the clock, eleven fifty nine, way past her bed time, Henry had long ago given up and went to bed without her.

Even though she didn't have to go to the pet shop in the morning she was to meet Jeremy at eight at the local Denny's. She quietly brushed her teeth and climbed into bed with Henry, he was growing fast and for some reason he thought he owned her bed, she scooted the snoring dog over to make more room for herself and in no time at all she was snoring right along with him. However her sleep was short lived, the beast of a cougar was back and he was meaner than ever, she was so disturbed that she could not go back to sleep, she didn't want to go back to sleep so she got up and did something she normally wouldn't do, she cleaned her house, she discarded all of the out dated food from the refrigerator and the pantry, leaving her nothing but a box of saltine crackers, three cans of tomato sauce, a package of Oreo cookies and a bag of Purina dog food and three bottles of water. She would definitely have to make a trip to the grocery store as soon as possible. She vacuumed and dusted, she sneezed-a lot. She moped and by the time she had finished with that it was time to get a shower and meet Jeremy.

*

Jeremy sat in a back booth at Denny's tapping his fingers impatiently on the table as he waited for Allison, he looked at his watch again, fifteen after eight, he sometimes wondered why on earth some people could not get anywhere on time. He looked up from his watch to see Allison strolling in acting as if she didn't have a care in the world. She looked around finally spotting him, she waved to him. He gave her a nod.

He noticed her large bag that she lugged over her shoulder and couldn't help but wonder what she could have in it and why she needed to carry so much of it, she walked towards him and tripped over her own feet, she didn't fall but she came close to taking out the waitress.

"Sorry." She apologized to her before slipping into the booth across form Jeremy.

"Your late."

"Good morning to you too."

"I don't like waiting on people."

"Like your never late for anything."

"No, I'm not late…ever." He stated, matter of factly.

"Sorry." She said again. "I had a rough night."

"Why?"

Before she could answer the waitress appeared to take their order, it was the same waitress that Allison had almost tripped.

"I'll have bacon, scrambled eggs, home style hash browns and wheat toast, with coffee."

"And you sir?" She asked Jeremy in a drippy sweet voice.

"I'll have the same." He winked at her.

"I'll have it out in a few minutes." She took the menus from his hand never taking her eyes off of his face. Allison was even sure that she winked at him as she walked away.

"Can you believe that?"

"What?"

"She winked at you."

"No she didn't."

"I saw her, she was flirting with you right in front of me." Obviously she hadn't seen him wink first.

"What difference does it make?"

"I could be your wife, or your girlfriend."

"But your not."

"She doesn't know that."

Jeremy was flattered, she was jealous. He knew she wouldn't admit to it but she was.

"Let's get back to business, you said you had a bad night, tell me why."

"I had night mares of the cougar again."

"What cougar?"

"Didn't I tell you about those dreams?"

"If you did I don't remember, so tell me." He stared into her eyes.

"I keep having dreams of a cougar attacking me, usually it's not really me but like I'm in someone else's body, I'm sure that the cougar represents the killer we are looking for."

The waitress set their plates down and Allison immediately picked up a strip of bacon, she was famished after all the house cleaning she had done in the wee hours of the morning.

"As I was saying, the cougar was mean but last night he was more aggressive."

"If he represents the killer how can he get more aggressive than murder?"

Allison waved her bacon in his face. "I think your killer is about to get more brutal, there will be more blood shed."

"You Don't think the next will be strangled like the others?"

"No, he's done with that I'm sure of it." She took one last swig of coffee before sliding out of the booth behind him.

"Where to from here?" She asked him.

"To the office, do you have a car?"

"Yes."

"Then I'll see you there." He climbed into a maroon Ford Explorer and drove away. He watched her in his rearview mirror she looked like she could have been angry, if she was she sure was cute when she was angry. He chastised himself for thinking about her like that, just because he found her physically attractive didn't mean that they had anything in common, it didn't mean that he should ask her out, it simply meant that she was cute, he wouldn't go as far to say she was smoking hot like Captain Johnson said she was, but she was cute.

Allison jumped into her ford focus and sped to catch up to him, she could see his eyes go from the road to the mirror.

"I know your watching me, I have my eye on you to mister." She sais aloud.

She followed him into the station parking lot parking next to him. He got out of his car and pointed to the sign. " That's a reserved spot."

She put her hand over the name plate. "Don't worry about it, Jack Monroe won't be needing his space today."

"And why won't he?"

"He's on a beach somewhere."

Jeremy grinned at her and her heart skipped a beat. " You can tell he's on a beach by putting your hand on his name?"

"It works for me."

"Ha." He pulled open the door allowing her to go in first.

"Keep your eyes off my butt detective."

"I don't know what your talking about Ms. Kramer." He lied, he had been checking out her perfectly round behind, but he would never admit to her.

"Your late Lottle." Captain said as he stopped by his office to check in. He looked up from his computer screen.

"I took your pet project out for breakfast and it set us back on time."

"How is Ms. Kramer?"

"She's ok."

"Smokin hot right?"

"I wish you would stop saying that, you sound like a horny teen age boy."

"You saying she isn't hot?"

"I'm saying she's ok."

"What ever, so you have a big day planned?"

"I don't know what we are doing just yet."

"Well figure it out, your getting no where standing here."

"Yep, by the way, is Jack Monroe coming in today?"

Captain was back to his computer. "Jack, no he took the family to Hawaii this week, why you ask?"

"Is there any way that Allison would have known that?"

"No, what's the matter Lottle? Her abilities starting to scare you?"

"Allison Kramer has yet to prove anything to me."

The captain laughed at him, it made his blood boil when people laughed at him. He could say some things that would make him mad to, like tease him about his name, Don Johnson, same as a television detective, what was that show called? Miami Vice. He saw Allison poking her head out of his office looking for him. He walked to where she stood. "What did you say?"

"Miami Vice, that old tv show. Don Johnson played Sonny crocket or was he Tubbs? I don't know which one he played." Allison said.

"Why would you bring that up now?" Was she reading his mind?

"I was waiting on you and the thought just came to me that your captain has the same name as the actor, and they are both detectives. Well the other Don Johnson only played a detective."

"I bet he wishes he looked like the other Don Johnson."

"I think our Captain is kinda cute."

"Since when is he OUR captain, and he sure as hell isn't cute."

"If your done putting the man down can we get down to business?"

"You started it."

Allison sat down in one of his overstuffed chairs and propped her feet up on his desk. He looked down at the worn out shit kickers on his clean desk and shoved her feet back to the floor. "Do you mind?"

"Sorry, just trying to get used to the place."

"If I were you I wouldn't get to comfortable."

"Fine, fine." She pulled a manila envelope from her giant purse catching his attention once again.

"What could you possible need so bad to warrant carrying a purse that large on a daily basis?"

"Not that it's any of your business but there are a lot of things I need in here on a daily basis."

"It looks like you have everything but the kitchen sink."

"Don't worry about it Jeremy." She dropped the bag back on the floor and opened the envelope up to display the pictures that she had taken home the night before.

"Did those help you have any miraculous visions last night?"

"No."

"I didn't think so."

"Stop being so negative Lottle."

"Excuse me."

"For what?" She asked thumbing through the files halfway ignoring him. " I want to go to the scenes of the crimes now."

"Right now?"

"Yes." She shut the folder, picked up her bag and headed for the door.

"Would you like me to go with you?"

"Yes, would you like to step on it?"

"What's your hurry lady?"

"You're the one who has been nagging me about some clues, so lets go find some clues big boy."

She turned away before Jeremy could see her smiling at her own remark.

"I'm driving." He said.

"Fine." She hustled to the explorer hearing the door unlock from his remote she slung the door open wide and jumped in, she heard paper under her and reached down to see what she had sat on, she pulled out a pack of cigarettes. "This is a bad habit." She scolded.

"I quit, those are old." He didn't look at her.

"It doesn't look like you quit."

"I don't care what it looks like nosey britches." He tried to grab them out of her hand but she rolled the window down and tossed them out onto the ground.

"Why did you do that?"

"Because, you said you quit so what difference does it make?"

"You had no right to do that and besides you just littered, that's against the law you know."

"Sorry." She stepped out of the explorer and picked up the pack of cigarettes, walked about thirty feet and tossed them into a trash can.

"There, is that better?" She asked dusting her hands off.

"No, it's not better because your making me want to smoke right now."

"It's all in here." She thumped on his head.

"Ouch, stop touching me."

"Are you always so testy?"

"No, I guess it's just you." He stepped on the gas and headed towards the Bakersfield college campus, speeding around the curves of panama lane.

"Slow down, I'm getting sick."

"Too bad." He smiled to himself. Would serve her right for throwing out his smokes, not that it had mattered, he had found those under the seat, no telling how old they were. He had no intention on smoking them, he had just forgotten to throw them out.

"I'm serious, I'm about to puke all over your dash."

"Calm down, we're here."

"Thank you Lord."

Jeremy shook his head at her dramatic antics.

"Are you always so dramatic?"

"No, I guess it's just you that brings it out in me."

Allison headed for the dorm rooms even thought she didn't know which one she was supposed to be going to. She looked back at him. "I would have thought with legs that long you could keep up better than that." She brushed her long hair away from her face, her blue eyes sparkled at him, his heart pounded and when she turned back around he quickly rearranged his pants, his body was starting to betray him, oh Lord help him, he didn't want to fall for this woman.

Ten

Rustling winds showed up on Destiny's caller ID at three in the morning, she reached blindly for the phone. "Hello."

"Destiny?"

"Yes."

"This is nurse Williams with Rustling winds mental health center, I'm sorry to wake you but I was to inform you of any problems we might have with—"

"Dustin, is he all right?"

"Dustin is sound asleep but your mother is carrying on about Dalana."

"I don't understand, Dalana is dead."

"I know that but your mother is talking as if she were alive."

"She's talking? She hasn't spoke a word since Dalana died."

"I know but she is carrying on now and I thought you might want to know."

"Thank you for calling but I don't know if there is anything I could do to help her."

"So your not going to come see her?"

"Not right this minute, I'll be there later today."

"Fine." The nurse said in a cool tone.

Destiny couldn't go back to sleep she couldn't stop thinking about that phone call. Why had her mother decided to start talking again, she had been pretty much comatose since they buried her sister, something would have had to spook her pretty good to get a rise out of her.

*

Allison slowed down so that Jeremy could take the lead. He led her to Stacy's dorm room. The room was the same as it was the last time he had seen it.

"It's hot in here."

"It's been closed up tight since we removed her body."

"I feel sorry for the next girl that get's this room." She told him. She walked over to the bed and sat down on the edge of it, running her fingers along the edge of the mattress she got chills. Jeremy leaned against the wall and watched her closely, there was something strangely erotic about the way she was moving. She lay her head back where a pillow would have been if they hadn't taken it in as evidence, she closed her eyes and suddenly she could see Stacy, sitting at her computer desk, her laptop opened up in front of her.

She was alone in the room but she was smiling, Allison felt as if she were right there in the room with Stacy. There was a knock on the door, Stacy opened it up. Allison could see another girl standing there, her face angry, her mascara running. She said something but Allison couldn't make out the conversation. The girl pushed Stacy aside so that she could enter the room. Allison jerked as Stacy fell backwards catching herself before she fell. This other girl was Jill Drake, she now recognized her from the photo. Jill went to the computer and pointed at it, they argued about something, Allison could barely make out an e mail on the screen. Stacy then picked up the laptop, closed it and shoved it into Jill's hands, then she took her by the arm and led her to the door all but forcing her out into the hall. She slammed the door shut. Allison jerked again and sat up from the dead girls bed.

"Well, what happened?"

"Stacy had a laptop, she and Jill argued about something on it, an e mail I believe and then Jill left with the laptop."

"I thought you might come up with something that might actually help me out."

"It doesn't."

"Actually, it's strange that you should mention e mail, Janice Deets called me and said that she found some printed out e mails in a notebook that Jill had left behind in her room from a study night."

"And?"

"She is supposed to bring them to the station this morning, actually yesterday morning."

"Then we should get back and be there to see her."

"Maybe she hasn't left yet, we could save her a trip."

Allison followed Jeremy down the hall, there were very few girls around, most of them were probably still out on vacation not done celebrating the new year, it was after all three more days before classes resumed. Jeremy stopped in front of Janice Deet's room but before he could knock the door opened and a stunned Janice stared at him.

"Detective Lottle, Did I misunderstand? I thought I was coming to you."

"I was in the neighborhood so I decided to come by and see if I could catch you before you left."

A wide smile crossed her face.

"Come in."

Jeremy took a step inside revealing Allison who had been behind him. Janice's smile fell, Allison caught it but Jeremy had been oblivious. "Who are you?" She asked Allison.

"I'm Allison Kramer detective Lottle's partner."

"I thought you said you worked alone."

"I do, I usually do but Allison has been assigned to help on this case."

"I see." Janice pulled some papers out of her bag and handed them to Jeremy. "These are the emails I found in the note book."

"Thanks."

Allison wondered around the small room, she ran her hand over the bedspread. "This is nice." She told Janice.

"Thanks, it was a gift."

"Oh from who?" Janice ignored her question and turned her attention back to Jeremy.

"If you don't mind, I have a lot of things to get done today so I'm going to have to ask you to leave." She crossed over and held the door open.

"We understand, and thanks for these, they may help us in some way." He shook the papers in his hand.

"Nice to meet you Janice." She held out her hand to Janice, she hesitated but shook it limply, then shut the door in their faces.

"Did I do something wrong?" Jeremy asked.

"Yes, you brought me."

"What are you talking about?"

"She has a crush on you Jeremy."

"She's just a kid."

"A kid with a crush on you."

"I don't think—"

"Yeah, yeah, I know but listen. The killer has been in that room."

"You Don't think Janice is the killer do you?"

"No, but the killer has been in that room I am sure of it."

"Do you think she's in on it? Partners in crime?"

"I don't know but willingly or not she has been in contact with a killer."

"I should warn her."

"No." She pulled him back.

"What if she is in on it, you can't give up anything we find out."

"But what if she is in danger."

"Tough decision, but I think we should wait and take the chance. I don't feel that she is in danger."

"If you feel that strongly about it. But nothing better happen to that girl."

He headed back to the explorer leaving her behind, she could feel Janice watching her when she turned back to her dorm room she saw the door close and heard a barely audible click as the latch caught. A horn honked and Allison knew that it was Jeremy waiting impatiently for her. She ran back to the car and hopped in. "Come on, you haven't been waiting that long."

"Long enough to read the e mails." He tossed the papers into her lap.

Stacy,

I love the pics that you sent me, can't wait to see you in person I'm sending a package, I want you to wear what's inside when we meet.

Tom

The next one read the same except for that it was addressed to Jill.

"Well, this is interesting, same e mail to two different girls both from Tom."

"And I 'll bet his last name is wall, only the real Tom Wall didn't write these, I believe a kid named Jim Gunner did.

"And who is Jim Gunner?"

"He's a kid we found dead on the football field night before last."

"Just a hunch."

Jeremy turned the car around and headed back towards the campus.

"Where are we going now?"

"Back to campus, I forgot to return this." He pulled the yearbook out from under the seat and handed it to her. "Look at the page that's ear marked."

She opened the book and turned up her nose. "Tom Wall is butt ugly."

Jeremy laughed out loud. "That's nice."

"Well I'm sorry, but it's true this boy looks like he was beat with an ugly stick—twice."

"Your too much Allison."

"So are you thinking that because this kid is so ugly he couldn't have wrote those e mails and couldn't be a killer?"

"If you were those two girls would you give this kid the time of day?"

"No, but maybe he's a sweet talker and sent them a picture of a different guy and when he showed up instead and things didn't go his way—you know the rest."

Jeremy pulled up in the circle drive in front of the school office. "I'll be right back."

Allison read another e mail while she waited for him to return.

Stacy,

R u sure no one else knows about our date? I can't risk being
seen in the girls dorm, promise me no one knows. Promise
you will tell no one.

Again the next one was identical addressed to Jill. Wow! She thought
to herself putting the pages down on the seat, she stared out the window.

*

"Mr. Lottle, this page has an ear mark, it was not that way when you
took it."

Jeremy leaned on the counter and gave the woman a playful wink. It
was not the same woman who had let him take the book but she knew all
about him having it. "That flirting may have worked with Ms. Taylor but
it will not work with me."

"I'm sorry, it was a thoughtless thing to do."

"I despise people who destroy school property and show no remorse
at all."

"I said I was sorry—Bernice." He read off her name tag.

"Sorry does not put this page back to the way it was now does it?"

"No Mam."

"Do not expect to take anything out of this library again Mr.
Lottle."

"That's a bit harsh don't you think?"

"No I do not and this conversation is over." She turned away from
him, leaving no choice but to walk away. He wondered if Bernice was that
way with every one or if he were just lucky.

He opened the door to the explorer and climbed in obviously catching Allison off guard.

"What are you humming?"

"Different strokes." It's an old television show.

"I know that."

"Then why did you ask?"

"Just wondering what made you hum that particular tune."

"I couldn't sleep the other night so I got up to watch a little tv and that's what I watched."

"Really?"

"Yes, Really." What was the big deal about her watching different strokes?

"I just think it's funny that we ended up watching the same show when we couldn't sleep."

"You too?"

"Yep!."

They sat in silence the rest of the ride to the station. Allison was relieved that it finally seemed as if Mr. Lottle was warming up to her.

Eleven

Destiny was reluctant to visit her brother today mainly because of the strange things that had been happening lately, her brother being afraid of her and then the call last night of her mother carrying on about her dead sister Dalana. She had not spoken or even acknowledged anyone since her death. As she came closer to Rustling Winds she could hear sirens behind her, they were getting closer, she had a knot in her stomach, panic set in and when the three police cars and one ambulance passed her she began to run, she tried to get into the building but an officer held her back.

"My family is in there, you have to let me in."

"No miss, they are bringing out an injured person and your in the way."

An injured person, she quietly prayed that it was not Dustin. She stood to the side and waited. When they wheeled the stretcher out she gasped, she never thought it might be her mother that was injured. She broke past the office and ran to her mothers side.

"Mom, Mom." Vanessa Gamble held her usual blank stare but she did speak one word.

"Dustin." Then she went limp.

"What happened in there, where is my brother?" She needed answers, she demanded answers.

Nurse Sonny approached her and led her to a concrete bench, she pushed Destiny down onto it and sat beside her. " At lunch time when the orderly went to get Dustin he was not in his room, so they went to your mothers room, they found Dustin standing over her with a bloody knife."

"No." Destiny was in shock, he would never harm anyone especially his own mother.

"I don't believe he did it."

"I know you don't want to believe it but it looks like that's what happened."

"Just because he had a knife in his hand does not mean he stabbed her."

"But that's how it looks, and until some one can prove different Dustin will be moved to a secure mental hospital for the criminally insane in Bakersfield."

"No, its jail, he didn't do it." She stood up and paced.

Two officers led her brother out of the building in a straight jacket, he was crying. She ran up to him and hugged him, wiping the tears from his eyes. "I'll be to see you as soon As I can." She promised.

He gave her a blank stare and muttered something that sounded like Dalana did it. Was Dalana haunting them, it made no sense why all of a sudden her sister was back in every ones mind.

"Does he have to be in a straight jacket?"

"Yes he does, he is a danger to himself and others."

"Miss Gamble." Destiny turned to see a good looking young officer. " If you need a ride I can take you to Delano Hospital to be with your mother."

Destiny read his name tag M. Guintoli. She would have refused but since she did not have a car and Delano was six miles away she decided to accept his offer.

"Thank you officer Guintoli, that would be nice."

Officer Guintoli held the door open for her, he said he would be happy to take her on to Bakersfield after he was off duty but she declined the offer, he had done enough for her and she didn't want to take advantage.

She approached the hospital and saw her father leaning against the wall with his back to her, he was on his cell phone and she heard him say. "How long before we can get the death certificate? Because I could really use the money that's why."

Destiny knew immediately what it was about, he was wanting the life insurance money, she knew he'd had at least a million on her mom, and she knew that he had a hundred thousand on each of the children. He'd bought a shiny new corvette with the insurance from Dalana's death. She was disgusted with the man, she couldn't believe that she once thought he was the best person in the world and she once loved him with all her heart. It was not so long ago that her family was together and happy but for the last six years it was like she was living some one else's life. A terrible life.

Destiny brushed past him entering the hospital, she made her way to the morgue where they allowed her to see her mother, she looked so peaceful, she almost had a smile on her face. She touched her mothers cold pale cheek and ran her fingers through her hair, she wished that she could have done more to help her throughout the past year but she was so far gone that she wouldn't let anyone break through the barrier. There was nothing more that she could do for her mother but hopefully she could help Dustin. On her way out the door her father grabbed her arm and held her so that she would have to talk to him.

"That hurts." She tried to get out of his grip.

"I'm sorry, but I have to get you to listen to me."

"Why should I listen? You Don't care about any of this family and you haven't for a long time. All you care about is mom's insurance money."

"You only heard part of the conversation."

"I heard all I need to hear, you have not been around for any of us since Dalana died-"Don't say her name."

"Why not? Why did you hate her so much?"

"I didn't hate your sister, I just couldn't look at her the same after—"

"After what? Tell me."

"I can't talk about it."

"Why not, she is dead, mom is dead and Dustin is crazy, why can't you tell me? don't you think I deserve some answers?"

"You do, but I can't give them to you."

"Why not?"

"Because I just can't." He snapped at her making her take a step back.

"I'm so ashamed of my actions, I'm sorry, so sorry." Tom Gamble sank to the ground in a heap and cried like a baby. Destiny wanted to comfort him but she couldn't bring herself to do so. "I have to see Dustin Dad, they think he stabbed mom."

Tom sniffled and wiped his face. He stood up and hugged his daughter. "You always took good care of your brother, he is lucky to have you."

"Will you be all right?" She asked, not really caring.

"I'll be fine, you go to Dustin. Here, take the car." He shoved the keys into her hand.

"How will you get home?"

"I'll make it there don't worry, I need to see your mother one last time and get the arrangements made."

Destiny turned away but then turned back to him. "Dad, do you think Dustin killed her?"

"If They hadn't found him in her room with the bloody knife I wouldn't have believed it."

"I still don't believe it." She walked away.

Destiny climbed into her Dad's corvette and headed to Bakersfield where they had taken her brother. Officer Guintoli had warned her that this place was nothing like Rustling winds which had a sort of country club feel about it, she mentally prepared herself for the worst.

*

Jeremy held the door open for Allison, she went into the office and flopped down into the overstuffed chair she had sat in earlier. "You really like that chair don't you?"

"I love it, I bet I would sleep like a baby in this thing."

"Yeah, well don't even think about sleeping, we have work to do."

Allison burrowed down further into the chair thinking a short little nap wouldn't hurt anything, she closed her eyes.

Jeremy noticed how long her eye lashes were, long and thick. She wore little make up, she didn't need it, her skin was virtually flawless, he was so lost in the sight of her that he hadn't noticed her eyes were now open and she was watching him study her, she said nothing but started when she saw that some one else was also watching her. Jeremy's eyes followed hers to the door. "Can I help you officer Sampson?"

"No I was just passing by." He put his head down and continued on his way. He still made Allison uncomfortable, but she wasn't sure why. She shivered.

"Are you cold?"

"No, I just got goose bumps when I saw him watching me."

"I haven't really cared much for the kid myself since he started working here."

"Something is not right with him Jeremy, I'd bet money on it."

"When you figure it out madam psychic will you let me know."

"I will, you will be the first to know."

She settled back into the chair and closed her eyes again, this time she was quickly asleep and Jeremy did not have the heart to wake her up. To pass the time he opened up the case file that had been dubbed the red velvet murders by the media He was sure that Jim Gunner was a part of this crime only because they did find a piece of red velvet on his body, but if he had been the guy pretending to be Tom Wall or if Tom Wall had actually written those e mails he still wasn't sure. He made a few more phone calls trying to be as quiet as he could so not to wake up his sleeping beauty, he crept up to her and wiped the drool from her chin, she blindly reached up and grabbed his hand, he thought he had been caught but just as quickly as she had grabbed him she released him, he sighed. All he needed was for her to wake up and catch him wiping drool off her face not only would that be embarrassing for him but also for her. The phone rang making him jump, he grabbed it before it could ring twice. "Hello—yes this is detective Lottle—are you sure? Thanks." Allison stretched letting out a little moan and making her breasts strain against her blouse. It was the sexiest thing he had seen in a long time.

"How long was I out?" She asked.

"About forty five minutes."

"Wow! I apologize. Why didn't you wake me up?"

"You looked so innocent not to mention quiet, I didn't want to wake you."

"Thank you, I really did need that cat nap."

"And while you were sleeping I found out that Tom Wall—the real Tom Wall passed away last year."

"How?" She was surprised.

"I would have thought that you might know that, considering you talk to dead people and all."

"How did he die? " She asked again, ignoring his pun.

"Car accident, he was driving home in a storm and hydroplaned into oncoming traffic, he was the only casualty."

Allison looked down into her lap. "What's wrong?"

"I feel bad."

"It wasn't your fault he died."

"I know but the cracks I made earlier about the ugly stick."

"Don't beat yourself up over it, you didn't know."

"But had I have know, I would never talk ill of the dead."

"I'm going to get us something to drink, I'll be back." She watched him walk to the vending machine, he was probably the best looking man that she had seen in a long time.

"Allison." She jumped up from the chair bashing her knee on Jeremy's desk.

"Captain Johnson, you scared the crap out of me."

"Why? Did I catch you staring at detective Lottle's rear end or something." He laughed at his own joke.

"Yes, but don't tell him that, his ego is big enough." She whispered.

"I'll keep your secret, how is your case going?"

"Slowly, we are working on some new leads right now."

"Great, keep me posted Kramer."

"Will do captain." He turned around and almost ran right into Jeremy. He laughed again and whispered something to him, Jeremy gave him that sideways grin she was growing to like. He came back into the office and kicked the door shut behind him, he handed her a sprite while he popped the top open on a coke and took a big swig causing him to burp loudly. His face turned red with embarrassment.

"Nice, but I think I can beat that." She told him.

"I'd like to hear you try."

"I wouldn't want to put you to shame." She took a sip of her drink, he thought she was joking but she could let out a burp better than any man could. "So what did Johnson say that was so funny?"

"Nothing." He could barely keep a straight face.

"Apparently it was something." She took another drink.

"Ok, if you must know, he said that you were staring at my butt."

Allison almost spit soda out of her nose. That rat said that he would keep her secret and he ratted her out within seconds.

"And you believed him?"

"Sure, I know I have a great ass."

"Oh please you are so—"

"So what?" He waited for her to finish what she was saying but she was staring off into space and there was nothing he could do except wait until she returned to reality in her own time. The tension drained from her body. "We are looking in the wrong town."

"What do you mean?"

"We have assumed that our killer was here in Bakersfield and he may be but our answers will be found elsewhere."

"Like where?"

Allison pulled out the picture of the group of cheerleaders. "Where was this picture taken?"

"I'm not sure."

"Well, find out."

Jeremy pulled out Jill Drake's parents phone number and asked where

she had attended high school. "McFarland high, McFarland—thanks."
He hung up right as a Allison said "Cougars."

"What about them?"

"That's why I was having dreams about cougars, They must be the
mascot for McFarland."

"Maybe it's just a coincidence."

"I don't think so, It's connected I'm sure of it. I told you we should be
looking in a different town and now we know which one."

"If we go now, by the time we get there it will be after school hours.
We may not be able to find anyone to give us any information." Allison's
shoulders drooped.

"Your right, we should wait until morning. But we leave first thing."

"You Don't have to tell me twice sister, I'm more anxious to find this
creep than you are."

"All right then, walk me to my car please."

"Why? It's not even dark outside."

"Humor me will you."

Jeremy acted like walking her to her car was putting him out in some
way but actually he was about to offer to walk her before she had even
asked. He grabbed his car keys and shut the light off. There was no reason
for him to stick around either, it was almost four and nothing they could
do until morning. Allison seemed sure that the answers they Were seeking
were in McFarland, thirty minutes north of Bakersfield.

"Do you like animals Jeremy?"

"Where did that come from?"

"I own a pet shop."

"I believe Cap told me that, yes I guess I like animals, I don't have any
pets of my own."

"Why not?

"I just don't have the time to take care of any, that wouldn't be fair to any animal."

"No it wouldn't be." He cocked his head sideways reminding her of Henry who did the same thing when he wasn't sure what she was talking about. She giggled.

"Why are you laughing at me?"

"Oh, I'm not laughing at you Jeremy it's just that—"

There he was giving her that crooked grin of his again, she nearly melted, she didn't know what was wrong with her, letting a man get to her like Jeremy did. She should turn and run now, spare herself any hurt. The last time she let herself fall for a guy he broke her heart. She didn't want to deal with that again. Dillon had said he loved her so many times but he just couldn't deal with the fact that dead people came to her for help, it finally was more than he could deal with and he left her.

"Hello, where did you go." He snapped his fingers in her face bringing her out of her trance. Nowhere, I'm still here."

"Good, I thought I'd lost you again."

"Not this time."

"Would you like to get something to eat?"

"Actually, I am hungry, we skipped lunch didn't we?"

"We just got busy."

"Yeah and that bacon and eggs we had for breakfast is about long wore off. I have to go home and check on Henry, I was going to do it during lunch but obviously I didn't get that done. He has been in the laundry room all day."

"Your gonna have a mess to clean up."

"I hope not. Henry and I have only been room mates for a few weeks. After the break in at the shop he just wasn't the same so I brought him home with me. Henry is the first animal I adopted myself."

"Really, I would think with you owning a pet shop that you would have a lot of pets, Henry must be special."

"He is, I don't just let any male into my home and heart. So do you want to pick me up at my place around seven?"

"At your place?"

"Yes." She rummaged through her bag until she found a business card and scribbled her address on the back of it. "I'll be ready when you get there."

"Does this mean I'm special?"

"What?"

"You said a male has to be special to get into your home and your heart."

"Don't get to cocky big guy, you haven't been in either yet."

She slid in behind the wheel and as the door shut he could have sworn that he saw NASCAR floor mats. Could it be, was she possibly a race fan. wouldn't that be something, none of the women he had ever been out with liked NASCAR, some would lie and say they did but when race day would come they were obviously put out at the thought of sitting for three to four hours watching a race with him. He still held hope that someday he would come across a woman that liked the same things that he did, he's still looking. He found himself in a good mood for a change.

"Lottle." Jeremy turned around to see Captain Johnson watching him closely. "I have to go out of town for a few days, call my cell if anything important develops."

"Will do."

"Have a good evening Lottle."

"I plan on that." By saying that he got Captain interested.

"What have you got planned?"

"I think I have a date."

"With Ms. Kramer I assume."

"Yes."

"I told you she has a hottie."

"Yeah, yeah, get on out of here Cap."

"See you in a few days."

"Have fun." Jeremy hadn't asked where he was going but he assumed when he saw Phyllis climb into the passenger seat of his car that they were going on a pleasure trip. He wondered if they were up to something, even if they were he didn't have time to think about it, he had to get ready for his date with Allison, he couldn't believe he was saying it, he couldn't believe he was doing it, but he was. He had really asked her out and she had accepted. If he didn't know better he would have thought he had butterfly's in his stomach.

Twelve

Destiny pulled up in front of a hospital that looked more like a prison, she double checked the address that officer Guintoli had wrote down for her. It was the right place, he did warn her that it would be nothing like Rustling Winds, it was a mental hospital for the criminally insane and it did make Rustling Winds look like a country club in comparison. There was no use in putting it off any longer she forced herself to get out of the car, walking along the narrow sidewalk to the double doors of the building, there were two security guards to greet her, they asked for her name and checked it against a list, she expected to be turned away because she hadn't called a head to get on any list but apparently some one had because they let her inside and pointed her to a desk. She had to walk through some metal detection stations first and some hairy goon had even insisted that he pat her down, she hadn't felt that was necessary. The woman at the desk was about as friendly as the guards had been, none of them had cracked a smile. She filled out a name tag and told her to put it around her neck. "Well, what are you waiting for?" The nurse asked.

"I don't know where to go." The woman breathed heavily as if she were agitated but she came out from behind the desk and led Destiny down a long spooky hall way the lights seemed to go dim every so often reminding her of a scary movie that she had seen last year, in the movie every time the lights dimmed was when some one was receiving electric shock treatment, she hoped that wasn't really the case. But she could hear people moaning and screaming all down the hall. She wondered how they might be treating her brother.

"Here is your brothers room, Ms. Gamble. There is a speaker so you can hear each other just fine."

"Your not going to let me in the room?"

"I can't do that, your brother is a danger to himself and others."

"He won't hurt me." Destiny truly believed what she spoke.

"I can't take that chance."

"You don't know my brother, he didn't kill mom, he wouldn't hurt a fly."

"Forgive me if I don't believe that, every one in here is here for attempting or actually killing some one."

"I understand." She gave up, it would do her no use to argue, the nurse was just doing her job and she couldn't fault her for that.

The nurse walked off and she pulled a chair up to the door, she sat down and was face level with her brother, he looked like he was spaced out on drugs, his eyes were vacant.

"Dustin, can you here me?" No response, not even a blink.

"Please." She pleaded. He ignored her pleas, she sat with him for three more hours until she heard a voice over the loud speaker saying that visiting hours were to end. She reluctantly stood and pushed the chair back against the wall where she had found it. She would have begged to stay all night if she thought Dustin would come around, but it wasn't looking good so she would just come back in the morning and try again.

"I love you Dustin." She thought she saw a hint of recognition but it might have just been her wishful thinking. She went back to the desk and returned her ID tag.

"Ms. Gamble, I didn't even realize you were still here."

"I'm all he has, and he is all I have. Where else would I be?"

"I assume you will be back in the morning then."

"Yes I will."

"Ok, visiting hours start at eight and I'll let the morning nurse know you will be back."

"Thank you." Obviously the nurses temperament had changed drastically since she had first arrived. Destiny drove a few blocks until she found a motel that looked descent, she showered and collapsed onto the bed falling asleep instantly. She was emotionally drained from everything that had happened.

*

Allison scurried around trying to figure out what she was going to wear on her date with Jeremy. She wasn't even sure if it was an actual date, she knew that they would be eating dinner but would it be a working dinner where all they talked about was the case or would work be off limits? They hadn't discussed where they would go so she didn't know how to dress. One thing she did know is that she was running out of time, it had taken her longer than expected to check on the pet shop and pay Louisa, she really missed the shop and all the little critters.

She had several different outfits laid out on the bed, the doorbell rang and there she stood in a bath robe, she tied it at the middle and went to the door.

He stood with her back to her. "Are you ready?" He said as he turned to face her. "I guess that's a no." He looked her up and down.

"Sorry I'm running a bit late." She looked him over, he was wearing jeans and a button down shirt, casual. That gave her something to work with. "Come on in, have a seat, visit with Henry and I'll be right back." She ran down a short hallway. Jeremy sat on the couch and looked around spotting a beagle pup peering at him from behind a chair. "You must be Henry." The pup crept out to lick his outstretched hand, he decided he was friendly enough and jumped up in his lap and begged to be petted.

Allison pulled a pink blouse over her head and pulled on a pair of relaxed fit jeans she quickly pulled her hair back into a pony tail, gave herself a once over in the mirror and was satisfied that she was ready. "I'm ready." She appeared in the doorway. Henry was now asleep across Jeremy's lap. "I kind of hate to move the little guy. Allison walked over to the couch and picked Henry up moving him into the doggy bed in the floor. Knowing that as soon as she left he would jump back up into her bed and keep it warm for her.

"So where are we headed?"

"I thought Applebee's and then maybe a game of miniature golf."

"Really?" She looked over at him curiously. He had no idea how good she was at that game, she played against many people and no one had ever beat her before.

"What, you don't like miniature golf?

"I'm not real good at it." She lied.

"I'll go easy on you." She tried to hide her smile.

As they pulled away from her house she noticed a grey sedan across the street but the driver turned away as they passed, she should have paid more attention to the strange car but Jeremy was her main focus for the evening.

As they ate dinner they talked about everything but work, they found out they actually had a few things in common, he was very pleased to know that she was in fact a NASCAR race fan, but he was less than thrilled with her choice of favorite driver, but at least he had a new friend that would gladly watch the race with him and not be bored, not to mention he did notice the sixty inch big screen in her spacious living room.

"I meant to tell you I like your house, it's big."

"I like big things." She stared straight ahead, that hadn't sounded good and she was sure he would take it the wrong way, when she dared to glance over at him he started laughing.

"Get your mind out of the gutter Jeremy Lottle, I was referring to things—like my television."

"I did notice that, I bet it's great on race day."

"You should come over Sunday and watch with me."

"This week is a night race on Saturday." He reminded her.

"That's right, I hate when they do that to me."

"Does the offer still stand or do you have other plans on Saturday night?"

Why didn't he just ask her if she had a date with some one.

"I do have plans."

"Oh." Was that disappointment in his voice she wondered.

"Your coming over to watch the race with me, I guess we can order pizza, do you like pizza?"

"Love it." He sounded relieved.

When they arrived at the golf course, as usual it was full of teen age testosterone but Jeremy wasn't about to let it stop him from having a good time with her.

"I should warn you Jeremy, not many people have beat me at this game."

"I thought you said you weren't real good at it."

"I shouldn't have lied to you, I am real good at it."

"Should I be concerned?"

"I just might beat the pants off of you."

"I should be so lucky." He mumbled.

"What?" She had heard what he said but she wanted to hear it again to be sure.

"I said don't bet money on it, I'm pretty good myself."

They played, they laughed and when it was all over He had beaten her by one point.

"First time for everything." He gloated passing their putts back through the window.

"We could go another round, I know, best two out of three."

"Another time, it's almost midnight and we have a busy day tomorrow."

"Rumor has it time flies when your having fun."

"I guess it's not a rumor, cause I had fun tonight Allison."

"So did I. Thank you!"

She found that her palms were sweaty and her tummy was doing flip flops. She wanted him to kiss her. He leaned towards her as if he would kiss her but two teen age boys rudely ran between them and the moment was lost.

"Punks." Jeremy called after them but they were oblivious.

"What kind of parents let boys that age run around this late? They couldn't be over fourteen. I was never allowed to be out past ten until I was eighteen."

Allison looked at him. "How old were you when you moved out of your parents house?"

"What do you mean, I still live at home." She was speechless, he was thirty something and still living at home.

"I'm just kidding, but my dad passed when I was seventeen and I went to school there in Bakersfield and then through the police academy, I was twenty four when I got my own place."

"You Don't have to explain anything to me."

"You asked."

"So how is your mom getting along with out you these days?"

"She is remarried and doing just fine, they are both retired and do a lot of traveling, they are in Kentucky right now."

"What's in Kentucky?"

"My uncle Phil."

"Oh, I see"

"Not for long, they are fixing to turn the lights out on us." He ushered her to the parking area, his explorer sat alone under a street lamp."

When they pulled up to Allison's house he walked her to the door, kissed her lightly on the cheek letting his soft lips linger for a moment but not long enough for her.

"Do you want to come in?"

"I shouldn't, it's late." She sighed with disappointment. Jeremy's watch made a beeping noise letting him know that another hour had passed. She unlocked her door and took a step inside. "Oh my gosh!"

"What?" Jeremy was reaching for the gun in his ankle holster.

"No, you don't need that."

"Then what are you oh my goshing about?" He put his pant leg back down.

"I just had a flash, a vision."

"Of what?"

"Captain Johnson and Phyllis in Vegas, at a wedding chapel."

"I saw them this afternoon, I knew they were going some where for a few days but I never would have guessed Vegas."

"I don't know why they didn't tell anyone, every one knows they are in love."

"Yep, they don't hide their affection very well."

"Well, I'm happy for them."

"Me too…. I'd better let you get some sleep, we have to get up before long."

"I'll be at the office about eight thirty if that's all right."

"That's fine, I'll see you then." He leaned in and pecked her on the cheek again.

"Bye." She closed the door. He waited outside to hear the lock click when it didn't he knocked again.

"Yes." She swung the door open wide.

"What is wrong with you woman?"

"I'm sorry."

"You live alone, and you open the door before you know who's knocking and then you don't lock it behind you as soon as you come in."

"I usually lock the door right away."

"I didn't hear it click."

"I had other things on my mind."

"Like what?" He asked.

"MMM, how about like wanting you to come in and take me in your arms and make mad passionate love to me. That's what she was thinking but she didn't dare speak her wishes out loud.

"Things, I promise I will lock the door this time." She shut the door he heard the click of the lock. " Now the dead bolt please." Hearing the dead bolt click he was satisfied. She watched him pull away from the curb, she snatched up her cell phone and texted her friend Teresa.

From Allison: Went to dinner with detective Lottle tonight.

Had a good time believe it or not, talk to you later.

She brushed her teeth and rinsed out her mouth, she heard her phone beep indicating she had a text, she'd expected Teresa to be asleep and not even get the message till morning. When she checked her phone she found that the message was from Jeremy.

From Jeremy: Had a great time tonight.

She giggled like a school girl

From Teresa: Did he kiss you?

From Allison: On the cheek

From Teresa: Bummer

From Jeremy: What is my pal Henry doing?

From Allison: Sleeping on my side of the bed.

From Jeremy: I wish I were sleeping in your bed.

She giggled again and forwarded the messages to Teresa so that she could read them.

From Teresa: damn girl, he is hot for you.

From Allison: I'm hot for him.

That text was supposed to be to Teresa but instead it went to Jeremy.

Jeremy smiled, she's hot for me huh?

Allison was so embarrassed she hoped he some how missed seeing that one but it appeared she wasn't that lucky.

From Jeremy: It appears you should do as I am and take a cold shower.

From Allison: good night Jeremy

From Jeremy: Sweet dreams Allison.

Thirteen

The next morning McFarland High school was crawling with teenagers, it seemed that they got there during a class change. Jeremy and Allison made their way to the principals office, she invited them in and was very accommodating and cooperative. Jeremy noticed the same picture of the group of cheerleaders that he had gotten from the Drakes house and now held in the evidence file. "Could I get a list of the names of these girls?"

"Sure, of course you already know two of them, Stacy and Jill."

"I'm well aware of that but I would like to know who the rest of them are."

Allison was focused on one girl. "Who is this?"

"That is Destiny Gamble, we had to boot her off the squad last week."

"Why?"

"Last year Stacy took Destiny under her wing and taught her everything she knew about being a cheer leader, she groomed her to take over—when she did take over the power seemed to go to her head and the other girls had had enough."

"From what I hear these girls think cheering is their life calling."

"For some of them it is detective Lottle."

"So I guess Destiny is pretty upset about getting released from the squad."

"Yes, but she doesn't need the added pressure of it anyway."

"Why is that?" Allison was curious to know more about this girl.

"Allison lost her sister in a car wreck just over a year ago."

"That's terrible."

"That's just the beginning, the accident made her mother and her brother nuts, the boy was always a bit off but this drove him over the edge."

"Poor girl."

"I'm not done yet, yesterday the boy stabbed his mother to death."

"Your kidding."

"No, it's nothing to joke about Ms. Kramer."

"No it isn't." She gave the principal a hard stare.

"Thank you for your time, we appreciate it."

"Any time Detective Lottle. Anytime."

Allison didn't like the way she was looking at him, she found the principal to be a bit Whorish, so to speak, what with her long legs, high hills and red lipstick.

"Can I ask you one more thing? Principal Kinney."

"Yes."

"What about the girls father."

"What about him?"

"Is he around?"

"He is, not much of a father though if you ask me, she handed him a list with the rest of the girls names on it, Jeremy thanked her again and the left the office. Walking down the hall Jeremy saw one of the girls from the picture only now she sported a cast on one leg.

"Excuse me, do you know Destiny Gamble?"

"I'm sorry to say I do." She answered.

"Don't get along with her huh?"

"She's the reason I have this on me." She gestured to the bulky cast.

"Sorry about that, do you know where we might find her?"

"Any other day I would say Rustling winds sanatorium but after what happened yesterday I doubt she would be there."

"Where is this Rustling Winds?"

"A few blocks up turn to the right, can't miss it really."

"Thank you, hope your leg heals fast."

"Me too."

*

They drove the few blocks to Rustling winds, it was easy to find from the school. "That poor girl, what she must be going through." Jeremy nodded in agreement. They pulled up through the entry of the facility, it must have sat on five acres of perfectly manicured lawn, the flower beds were amazing, and the three story brick building was immaculate.

"This place is beautiful."

"Yep, let's go inside and see what we can find out."

As they walked up to the door they passed a group all dressed in yellow shirts and orange shorts they carried butterfly nets and headed to the garden. "That looks like fun." Allison told Jeremy. "Maybe we can do that on our next date." Allison said nothing but her heart warmed at the thought of going out with him again.

Jeremy showed his badge to a woman who's name tag read Sonny Price.

"How can I help you?"

"I'd like to ask you a few questions."

"Didn't we answer enough questions yesterday?"

"I'm actually with the Bakersfield police department working on a case that might be related to what transpired here yesterday."

"You mean the stabbing of Vanessa Gamble?"

"Yes."

"Are you working on the case involving the dead co eds?"

"I can't say."

"You just did. Both of those girls attended high school here, they were both cheerleaders just like Destiny." She put her hand to her chest. Do you think that Destiny is in some kind of danger?"

"I don't know for sure."

"I hope not, she is such a sweet, sweet girl."

Funny, they had just heard the opposite from the high school principal and Lisa.

"Do you know Destiny well?"

"I'd like to think so, she has been here everyday for just over a year."

"I hear that her mother and brother were both here."

"Yes, after the accident that killed the sister Dalana, Vanessa lost all sense of reality and Dustin was not all there anyway but he became more withdrawn. He was found standing over his mother with the bloody knife in his hand—the kids are triplets, did you know that?"

"No, we didn't know that."

"Do you believe Dustin stabbed his mother?" The nurse hesitated.

"I don't know, I wouldn't have thought it at all but the fact that he was holding the murder weapon makes me wonder, I worked closely with that boy everyday. but strange happenings have been going on with that family in the last few days."

"What happenings are you referring to?"

"Dustin does not talk much at all except to Destiny and even then it's always in broken sentences, one night Dustin began carrying on about Destiny, he said that she scared him and when she showed up that day for her visit he wouldn't have anything to do with her."

"Odd."

"Very odd, even odder was the fact that Vanessa had showed some signs of activity that surprised us all, she had been here a year and never showed any recognition of anyone, we thought that maybe Destiny had shown up after hours and something happened that we didn't know about."

"And—"

"Well, she was as surprised as we were, she was shocked that her mother had shown any kind of recognition and she was devastated when her brother was scared of her. He finally came around."

"Do you know how we can reach Destiny?"

"I'm not allowed to give out any numbers or an address but I am sure that you will find her in Bakersfield at the Vine institution. That is where they took Dustin after the incident."

"I'm familiar with the place, it's a federal lock down for the criminally insane." Jeremy stood up ready to leave, he had all he could get from her. "Thank you for your time."

"Your welcome. anything to help those kids, I believe they are good children, they have just been through so much."

They got on the highway and down the road a little "Are you hungry?" He asked her.

"I was until we talked to that nurse."

He pulled off the highway and into a Jack In the Box drive through. She leaned over and whispered that she would have a taco and a coke.

"I thought you lost your appetite." "I can't ever turn down a Jack In the Box taco."

Jeremy place their order and got back on the road, she opened up his burger and wrapped it so that he could eat and drive, she took a bite of her taco and felt a drop of sauce travel down her chin. "You got something on your chin." He told her. "Yeah, I feel it." she wiped her face with a napkin and then looked over at him. " I don't know what your laughing at." She giggled, he looked in the mirror and saw sauce dripping from his own chin. She reached over and wiped his mouth for him. "Thanks."

"Don't mention it."

Jeremy's cell phone rang, he handed her his burger to hold so that he could answer.

"Hello, It's the office." He whispered. "I'm about twenty minutes away but I was already headed there." He hung up.

"What's going on?" Allison asked sitting up taller in her seat.

"Linda says a call came in from the Vine institution where Dustin is—"

"And?"

"You didn't give me a chance to finish."

"Sorry."

"Some one escaped from their room last night, no one has ever gotten out of one of the rooms from the Vine."

"Dustin?"

"Yep."

"How, I thought he was doped up and on lock down, or whatever they call it."

"Yes, but they still escape from prison once in a while don't they?"

"I suppose."

"So does this mean we are officially on the Dustin Gamble case?"

"Looks that way, now the McFarland police is going to have to share their information with us."

By the time they arrived at the Vine institution the place was crawling with black and whites as well as unmarked cars and the first person they saw was officer Sampson.

"There he is again, we can't get away from him."

"He is a cop Allison, he is going to be at a lot of crime scenes."

"I realize that, but he makes my skin crawl."

"He's not that ugly."

"No, he's rather good looking, but he's creepy, he's shady."

"Well, we have other things to worry about besides Sampson."

"Don't be to sure about that." He turned and looked back at her.

"Do you really think that Sampson is up to no good?"

"I don't have a good feeling about him at all."

"Ok, I'll check him out, but first we have to see what happened here last night."

At the front desk Jeremy once again showed his badge. " She's with me." He told the people at the desk when he saw they were reluctant to let Allison pass.

Another detective had gotten there first and had given them the rundown.

"This kid, seventeen year old Dustin Gamble was admitted here yesterday after allegedly killing his mother up in McFarland, they doped hip up and locked him in a room, he was almost in a vegetated state—so one nurse tells me. They say his sister was here with him for three or four hours and during that time he never acknowledged her existence, how ever they said that when the guard did his eleven P:M check that the kid was lucid enough to know that he was present and he was pacing the floor."

"Why didn't they keep him medicated if they had thought he was a killer and dangerous to himself? Jeremy asked. The other detective shrugged his shoulders.

"Your right detective, the boy should have been drugged to keep him calm. He shouldn't have had the strength to be pacing the floor much less find a way out of the room."

The woman speaking wore a nurses uniform, the name tag read M. Monks.

"What are you saying?"

She opened up a chart and read over it briefly. " I'm saying that according to what the doctor ordered for this boy he should have been much to heavily sedated to be pacing the floors."

"So who was responsible for giving him his meds last night?"

"That would have been nurse Lucy."

"Is there a chance nurse Lucy forgot to give them to him?"

"Doubtful, she doesn't forget much, but here she comes you can ask her yourself."

Allison asked if she could see Dustin while Jeremy talked to nurse Lucy nurse Monks led her down the hall to where Dustin's room was. She looked things over carefully. " I just don't see how he could have gotten out of this room on his own in the first place."

"I don't either Ms Kramer, it's never happened before, the kid must be some kind of Houdini."

Allison studied Dustin, his blond hair needed trimming, his skin was so pale but clear. He looked like a porcelain doll, she knew that right now he had been sedated but looking at him she just didn't see a killer.

Nurse Lucy showed Jeremy on her chart exactly when she had given Dustin his meds.

"Detective, I have worked here for twenty years, I know how important it is for these inmates to get their meds. I never forget and I always make sure they swallow them."

"I don't doubt that you are very proficient nurse Lucy but is it possible that he fooled you and hid the pills somewhere making you think that he had swallowed them?"

"Your officers searched that room up, down and sideways before we put him back in there and they found nothing."

"One more question, just between you and me, you said yourself you have worked here a long time. Do you think this kid is faking his mental illness?"

Jeremy heard high heels clicking behind him, It seemed as if someone was always sneaking up behind him, He turned to see a tall long legged red headed beauty staring at him.

"I'll take it from here Nurse Lucy."

"Yes Mam." Lucy scurried away like a scared little mouse. he had to admit even he was a little intimidated by this woman. "Karen Stone." She said holding her hand out to him. He shook it. "Detective Lottle."

"I'm the resident Psychiatrist." She walked over to a seating area and sat down, she crossed her legs making her skirt inch upward on her thighs. " I evaluated Dustin Gamble yesterday when he first arrived and I can assure you that the boy is not faking anything."

"Ok, but lets say he did take his meds and they were strong enough to incapacitate him how do you explain his great escape from the room?"

"You're the detective, do I really have to tell you that the only way for that boy to get out of the room was if some one let him out."

"Who would do that?"

"Once again, you're the detective."

"I'm going to need a list of all the past and present employees."

"I can get that for you." She ran her fingers up and down her legs in a seductive fashion. If he didn't know better he would have thought she was flirting with him.

"Was any one hurt here last night or is this all about him getting loose from the room."

He had to ask because it sure seemed like they were making an awful big deal about it.

"Need I remind you, the child killed his mother just hours ago. His being loose, roaming the halls could have resulted in some one else being hurt or even killed." He leaned into her. " Do you believe this kid killed his mother?"

"I think it's a good possibility."

"Rustling winds is full of people who aren't all there—sorry I'm not sure how else to put it."

"And your point detective?"

"It's possible that someone else could have killed Vanessa Gamble. Dustin could have came in after the fact and unknowingly picked up the knife. It doesn't mean he did it."

"It's possible he didn't, but likely that he did."

"Thank you Ms. Stone for your opinion."

He stood up and walked towards Allison. Karen Stone grabbed his hand, she held it in her own. "You have large strong hands detective."

"Uh, thanks."

"Would you like to go out some time?"

"Actually, I have a girlfriend and I don't think she would like that idea." He looked down the hall, his eyes met Allison's and he realized how much he cared for her, even though she wasn't technically his girlfriend after last night he knew that he wanted to spend a lot more time with her.

"That's her? The girlfriend."

"Yes."

"Lucky woman."

"Maybe I'm the lucky one."

"If it doesn't work out you know where to find me."

Jeremy walked up behind Allison and touched her shoulder, she shied away from his touch. "Who is the red head?"

"Resident psychiatrist."

"Oh, I thought she might have been a sex therapist the way she was all over you."

"You were spying on me?"

"I'm sure I'm not the only one who saw her sick public display of affection towards you."

"Calm down, doll face. She means nothing to me—you sound like a jealous girlfriend."

She gave him a look.

"I kind of like it." He added.

Allison turned her attention back to Dustin, his eyes still looked strange but they were now trained on her.

"Hello Dustin."

He blinked as if to say that he heard her.

Poor kid." Jeremy whispered in her ear."Every one thinks he is guilty."

"I don't." Allison did a double take, the girl who had spoke looked remarkably like Dustin, it could have only been one person, Destiny Gamble. They were darn near identical in looks. Except for the fact that she had longer hair and she wore make up. Even the make up couldn't conceal the dark circles under her eyes.

Dustin stirred a little bit, he mumbled something, surprising Allison considering she had been sitting and talking to him and he never stirred or tried to speak. The frail girl moved toward the glass door and her brother mustered up the strength to scoot back on his bed plastering himself against the wall, he was clearly afraid of her.

"It's me Dustin."

"Lana." He whispered.

"No, its Desty. Dalana is gone, she's dead."

"Saw her."

"No you didn't."

"Yes, saw her." He insisted.

"You must have been having bad dreams again Dustin."

"Does he have dreams about Dalana a lot?" Allison asked.

"He did right after the accident, he thought Dalana hid under his bed and would come out at night just to scare him."

"How long did those dreams go on?"

"About six months, he was finally getting where he was coming back to me, almost speaking in full sentences and now all of a sudden he thinks she is back, and he thinks I'm her."

"Did your mom ever have nightmares? Did she think Dalana was still alive?"

"Mom withdrew from the world, who knows if she had any thoughts or dreams. That's why I was shocked when they said that she had acknowledged one of the staff and of course before I could get there to see for myself…some one had killed her."

"You don't believe your brother did it?"

"No."

"You mentioned that Dustin was afraid of Dalana, why?"

"Dalana was mean, she hated me and she tortured him."

"A lot of siblings act like that during adolescence."

"Not like this, Dalana sometimes acted like she was pure evil, she hated me because Dad for some unknown reason hated her and I think the thing with her and Dad is why she acted the way she did. Mom knew that dad had time to save Dalana from the fire but he waited, he waited until the car exploded and there was no chance to save her."

"Are you saying that you think your Dad just let her die?"

"Yes, and that's what drove mom crazy, she knew that he let her die."

"What about your brother, is Dalana the reason he is—how he is?" Jeremy asked.

"Dustin had problems early on, he is mildly retarded but Dalana always called him retard and she would punch him when she thought no one was looking. I always thought Dustin would have been happy had it not been for Dalana's treating him the way she did."

All three of them turned their attention back to Dustin, he was staring intensely at Destiny and chewing his nails. "Desty?" He asked.

"Yes Dustin, It's me." She assured him.

He jumped up from the bed. "Desty, Desty." He pressed against the glass door.

"I love Desty."

"I love you too Dustin."

"No like Lana."

"She Can't hurt you anymore."

Dustin lifted his sleeve to reveal a large black and blue bruise on his arm, it was the same arm that Dalana would always punch him on.

"What happened Dustin. Who did this to you?"

"Lana." He answered.

Destiny turned toward Jeremy and asked him. "Why does he keep insisting that Dalana hurt him even though I keep telling him she is dead and can't hurt him any longer?"

"I don't know, but some one hit the boy and I will find out who is responsible for that."

"Thank you detective, will you also find out who killed my mother? Because I know that Dustin didn't do it."

"I'll do what I can, as long as the McFarland police department works with me on this and gives me all the information."

"I'll help you any way that I can." She offered.

"Great, you can start by telling me everything about your family, your life."

"Anything you want to know, may I suggest you start with my dad."

"Why with your Dad?"

"Because I think it might be a possibility that he killed mom, or had some one else do it."

"What would make you think that?"

"When I went to hospital morgue my Dad was on the phone with the insurance company and he was already trying to get a check from her life insurance policy. She wasn't even cold yet."

That didn't sound good. Allison shook Jeremy by the arm trying to get his attention.

"What is it?" He asked agitated.

"Look in Dustin's hand."

Jeremy and Destiny both looked, in his hand he held a little piece of red cloth.

The nurses timing couldn't have been better.

"It's time for Dustin's medication." She opened the slot in the glass door and slid in a cup containing two pills and right behind another cup with some water. Allison asked him if she could see what he was holding. He shook his head no. "Please Dustin, I would really like to see what you have."

It was almost as if he sensed that what he held may have been of some importance to her he stepped forward and put the piece of cloth through the slot to Allison. Jeremy quickly scooped up the cloth " Velvet." He said feeling of it.

"Where would he get that?" Destiny asked.

"I don't know." Jeremy said. But he did know, he knew that there must be another victim waiting to be found. A victim who had on red velvet and a piece of it missing.

"Thank you Dustin."

"Wel-come Allson." he told her in his broken speech.

"He likes you." Destiny seemed surprised. " It usually takes him a while to warm up to people but he seems to like you."

"He knows I'm not here to hurt him, only to help him. I know he is innocent and I'm going to help prove it so he can get back to his regular life, so he doesn't have to be afraid anymore."

Jeremy looked at her. Silently wishing her to be quiet, she shouldn't be telling Destiny any of this.

"We should be going, you have a good visit with your brother. We will be in touch."

"Thank you both."

"Your welcome, goodbye Dustin." Allison called out. He gave her a nod.

Jeremy grabbed her arm and walked her out.

Fourteen

Jeremy went straight to the car he didn't speak to her and he didn't look at her, he climbed in slammed his door shut started the car put it in gear and started rolling before she even had her door shut.

"What's your problem?"

"My problem? What's my problem?"

"Ok, I guess it's a hearing problem." She smiled at her own joke.

"There is nothing wrong with my hearing lady, however I wish I hadn't heard what you said to Destiny."

"What are you babbling about?"

"How are you going to prove that Dustin is innocent when you don't know that he is?"

"He is."

"You Don't know that."

"I feel it, I'm sure that he didn't kill anyone."

"Fine, you feel it, but please keep those feelings unspoken from now on."

He was almost yelling at her now. She sat back in her seat pulling the seatbelt around her, her feelings were hurt and Jeremy sensed that.

"I'm sorry Allison but there are some things that you just can't say out loud or in front of suspects, even if you think they are innocent."

"I'll just keep my mouth shut from now on."

"Don't be like that doll face." He stroked her cheek. She brushed his hand away.

"Don't call me doll face."

He decided it would be in his best interest to just be quiet, he tried to figure out how he could get into the Gambles house and look around with out a search warrant because truth was he had no just cause for a warrant, just a hunch that there might be something there.

"I'm sure if you ask Destiny she would let you look around in her house."

"There you go reading my mind again."

"I wasn't reading your mind, but I obviously was thinking along the same lines."

"Whatever you say doll face."

She just shook her head and continued to stare into her lap on the way back to the precinct. Wondering how he could go from angry to sweet in a matter of seconds.

"We should go to the dorm."

"Why?" She asked.

"Dustin had red velvet."

"Could be a coincidence."

"Who in that place would have on red velvet, he got it from some where."

"It could be a piece of ribbon or off a nurses coat, it could have came from anywhere."

"Come on Allison."

"They said there was no way he could have gotten out of the building, just the room, he didn't leave the property. He got that velvet from inside the building."

"You Don't know that for sure."

"He's being set up." Allison was sure of it

"That's a big assumption."

"Go to the dorm, your right we should check on Janice." She said.

"I'm sure she is fine."

"It was your idea in the first place, follow through on it and go check on her."

"Ok, I think I will call first and let her know that we are coming."

"Fine." She sat back in the seat.

Jeremy fumbled with his phone dropping it twice.

"Maybe you should call, I'm trying to drive."

Allison jerked the cell phone out of his hand and punched in the number. "Voicemail."

She told him. "Should I leave a message?"

"No."

Allison didn't want to be right about Janice but she knew that something was wrong, she had a thing for Jeremy and if she saw his number she would have answered it right away. It was dusk now as they made their way to the dorm rooms. They knocked on Janice's door, no answer. Jeremy's heart sank. He recalled Allison's words from days ago telling him that Janice should be warned. He Didn't think she was in danger at the time. Allison reached for the door knob.

"What are you doing?"

"Seeing if the door is unlocked."

"Better use this." He pulled out a handkerchief an wrapped it around the knob. It was unlocked.

"Stay put he ordered."

Allison rolled her eyes, he pushed the door open and slowly stepped inside. Allison was right behind him.

"You listen well."

"Thanks."

He rolled his eyes this time.

The room looked undisturbed—at first. "It looks like blood on the bedspread." She whispered in his ear.

Jeremy walked over to the bed, when he looked on the other side between the bed and the wall he saw her. Janice lay still in a pool of blood. She hadn't been strangled like Stacy and Jill, she had been stabbed like Jim Gunner and Vanessa Gamble. Allison stood behind him and gasped when she saw Janice.

"Go out in the hall and call 911." He told her.

While she was out there he had a few minutes to closer inspect the crime scene, he pulled out the piece of velvet that they had gotten from Dustin. It was a perfect match of the piece missing from Janice's underwear, upon closer inspection he noticed that even thou she had on red velvet like the others, the pattern was indeed different. Allison was now back in the room beside him.

"What do you think about the pattern being different?"

"Different killer."

"You think copy cat?"

"That or accomplice."

"Usually a serial killer does not change his methods, Stacy and Jill were strangled, Janice was stabbed, this was a messy kill, had to be a different person."

"Unless he is just trying to throw us off."

Jeremy was becoming so frustrated he wanted to pull his hair out."

"Allison, if we ever needed your psychic abilities we need them now. Give me some answers please."

"I wish I could just tell you who is responsible Jeremy, but it doesn't work like that, things just come to me in their own time."

"The right time would have been before Janice was killed."

"I knew we should have warned her." She said.

"We Didn't know who to warn her of."

"I know but if he had let her know she could be in danger maybe she wouldn't have opened her door for this person, maybe she could have went home and been safe."

"Allison, it's not your fault that she is dead."

"I know." But IT didn't stop her from feeling guilty.

"Dustin must have gotten out of the hospital last night."

"He Didn't do this, he couldn't have."

"How can you be so sure he didn't get out? How can you be so sure that he is innocent?"

"That's just how I feel."

"How do you explain the velvet found in his hand? In his hand, Allison."

"The only explanation I have for that is that he is being set up. You saw him, do you honestly think he has the mental capacity to get himself out of the room, the hospital, sneak into this dorm kill some one and get back into the hospital with out any one seeing him?"

"Maybe he is just that good of an actor, and escape artist" Jeremy suggested.

"Even if he could fool us, I don't think that he would be able to fool his sister."

*

The young officer Sampson stepped into his dark apartment, it had been a long drawn out day with having to deal with all the action at the Vine institution and Dustin Gamble, it still bothered him to see that kid but he needed to stay close and keep up with what was going on. He nearly passed out when he saw Destiny walk in, she looked so much like Dalana is was scary he barley held himself in check.

"Hi baby." came her voice from behind him, out of the darkness. Her thin arms wrapped around his middle and moved over his chest, he turned in her arms to face her. Her hair smelled like strawberries. "I missed you." He told her.

"I missed you too Bobby." He picked her up and carried her to the bedroom, he slowly discarded her nightgown and tossed it to the floor. As usual she tried to cover the scars on her torso, he pulled her hands away from her. "I love you just the way you are Dalana."

Fifteen

Allison and Jeremy sat in his office, he kept giving her a sideways glance that was frankly getting on her nerves, finally she confronted him about it.

"What? Why are you looking at me like that?"

"I don't know what your talking about."

"Like your mad at me because your not getting your way, because I can't just come out and tell you who killed those girls."

"And boy." He added.

"As I have said so many times before, I don't think Dustin is guilty. Especially after meeting him yesterday."

"If you want to know what I think—"

"I don't." She cut him off.

"Your going to hear it anyway, I think that you are getting to close to this creep, maybe even starting to like him a bit."

"Are you talking about the killer or Dustin?"

"Aren't they the same person?"

"Get over it Jeremy, I'm doing my best to help you get this figured out."

"There was a time when I believed that but now all of a sudden your trail has grown cold, why is that?"

"I don't know why I just haven't had any vibes or visions lately." She threw her hands up in the air.

Jeremy snickered. "Vibes, I knew this was a mistake, I told cap it wasn't a good idea but he insisted that you could help, well do you want to know what I think?"

"No, but for some reason you keep asking."

"I think your psychic ability is all a load of garbage, I think your just here to get close to me."

"I didn't even know you existed before I set foot in this place."

"But, since the first time you saw me you have wanted me."

"What an ego you have, I'm not here for you, I am here because your captain asked me to be here, he thinks I can help."

"Shows what he knows."

"You should be grateful." She grabbed her handbag and headed for the door, stopping suddenly, a grin spread across her face, she turned back, walked up to him. " If I really wanted to get your attention I would have just done this." She kicked him in the shin as hard as she could. And left his office.

He doubled over in pain, that hurt like a booger. He sank into a chair. "I'll get you for that." He yelled. "Bitch." He added under his breath.

Captain Johnson being back from his trip from Vegas had been watching from his office door. He crossed over into Jeremy's office. "What's all the yelling about?"

"Why don't you ask you psychic friend out there. I told you she would be trouble." He pulled his pant leg up and looked at the developing bruise she left from her shit kicker boots, he hated those boots. Captain wanted to laugh but contained himself.

"When I brought her in on the case we had no leads at all. Now at least we have some leads."

"But our prime suspect has some kind of hold on her and she refuses to believe that he could be responsible."

"That's your job to prove if he's guilty or innocent."

"I know what my job is." He snapped.

"I don't think this case is all that's bothering you."

"I've thought about nothing but this case for the past six weeks."

"She is a beautiful young woman."

"What?"

"Allison, she's beautiful."

"And your point being."

"I think you like her."

"She's a hell cat, look what she did to my leg, she kicked me."

Captain Johnson stuck his head outside of Jeremy's office, the office some of the other employees referred to as the torture room. Jeremy could be a bear at times.

"Get in here right now Kramer." He ordered, the entire room heard and Allison felt as if she were in school being called into the principals office.

"Sit down." he told her. She did as she was told even though she was less than thrilled at the idea of sitting in the same room with Jeremy. The man was almost impossible at times no wonder he worked alone, no one could stand him, it was also no wonder that he had never been married.

When Allison sat next to him she saw the goose egg that she had left on his shin, she smiled with self satisfaction.

"Now the two of you had better listen up. I want this nonsense to stop, your both acting like children, I thought you two were finally starting to get along, if not then you had better start because it's going to take both of you to catch our killer and you need to work together to do it."

"Maybe he's done killing. Maybe that's why her vibes have stopped."

"I've been trying to use my powers to contact—"

"Oh please." Jeremy cut her off. Standing up and looking down on her. "Use your powers to get in touch with this lady." He grabbed his crotch and watched as her face turned crimson.

"Show some respect Lottle or I'll throw you out on your ear."

Allison held up her hand. "That's all right Captain I can handle Lottle."

"Handle this lady." Jeremy said grabbing his crotch again."

"You should be careful what you wish for because it just might come true." Allison approached and placed her hand on his crotch her tender touch brought a smile to his face but it wasn't long until than tender touch became a painful squeeze. He grimaced.

"From now on detective Lottle I expect to be treated with the same kind of respect that you would show to any other partner that you might have had, the same respect that I have shown you, is that to much to ask for?"

"No." He replied in a slightly higher voice than usual.

"Great, now that we have established the fact that you can u hem! Handle Detective Lottle, can we please get back to work?" Captain looked out into the larger office where all eyes were trained on Allison and Jeremy. "That goes for the rest of you, get to work."

"I'll be back in the morning, maybe we will all be in a better mood." Allison told them before walking out of the room and then out the front door, her blond ponytail swaying behind her as she bounced across the floor.

Sixteen

Allison stood up straight standing in front of her bathroom sink, looking at herself in the mirror she began to babble about the great detective Lottle, just who the hell did he think he was? She didn't ask to be on this case she had been content on staying to herself she never would have offered to help if it hadn't been for Captain Johnson practically ordering her to do so, yes, he had treated her as if she were on the force and was obligated to be on the case. She had given Jeremy all the information she had every vision she had seen, anything that could help she had told him and yet all he did was joke and criticize her about her abilities, the truth was that with out her and her help he would have been at a complete loss. "It's not me that your pissed at, it's the fact that you can't figure it out for yourself." She yelled into to the mirror as if Jeremy were standing in front of her. She wanted to tell him exactly how she felt, what she thought of him. She left the bathroom and sat down on the side of her bed, she picked up the phone and dialed his number, it rang twice before she heard his voice. "Hello." He said in that deep sexy tone of his. She opened her mouth to speak but when nothing came out she hung up instead. He wasn't always a pain in the butt he had a soft side about him.

She went back to the bathroom sink and grabbed her toothbrush, she squirted a wad of toothpaste just as her phone rang, she jumped which made the paste miss her brush and land on the clean counter top instead. "Darn it." She put her brush down and went to answer the phone.

"Hello." She said angrily.

"Did you just call me?"

She froze. "No." She lied.

"Really? Are you sure?"

"Don't you think I would know if I had just called you?"

"I have caller ID, I know it was you."

"Darn it." She stomped her foot. How could she be so dumb not to even think he might have caller ID.

"So why did you hang up? Better question is why, did you call?"

"I decided it wasn't worth wasting your time."

" Since we are talking now why don't you let me be the judge of that."

"Never mind." She insisted.

"Allison." He prodded.

"I was just replaying all the times you have been a total complete ass to me and the more I think about it the more I don't like it."

"Is that so?"

"It is, I think you should just cool your jets and work with me just like you would any other partner you would have."

"But your not a real partner, your not a cop, your not a detective."

"But I am a human being with real feelings and you hurt them a lot."

"I don't always mean what I say, but listen here missy, if your going to work with the police you better get a thick skin and quick."

"I can't wait until this case is solved so that I can get away from you." She told him.

"Come on Ali, I may not be psychic but I can tell when a woman likes me." He giggled.

"Like you, I detest you Mr. Lottle."

"You want me and you know it, your just to stubborn to admit it."

Click

"Hello." She had hung up on him. She wants me. He said to himself.

Allison returned to the sink and once again attempted to put paste on her brush succeeding this time. She brushed so hard her gums bled, she gargled with mouthwash making her gums sting even worse. Oh that man made her so mad, she needed to cool off some how, a cool shower maybe. As the water cascaded over her naked flesh her thoughts could not escape the detective, he was right, she wanted him, for the life of her she didn't know why but he turned her on. She wondered what it would feel like to have his hands touch her body, to kiss her full lips. She shook off the thought. When she again heard the phone ring she thought it was Jeremy so she let the machine pick it up, it was him.

"Come on Allison, pick up the phone….please."

She didn't answer and the phone continued to ring. She dried herself off and slipped on a pair of shorts and tank top portraying the image of her favorite NASCAR driver, it was still early so she sat on the sofa and began to channel surf, as always there wasn't much on, the doorbell rang and without thinking she answered it. She stood in shock.

"So can I come in." Jeremy asked as he leaned against the door frame looking her over.

"I suppose, but one negative word out of you and your outta here."

"Ok." He agreed shutting the door behind him.

"Sit down."

"Yes Mam." He checked her out as she sat on the sofa in her little orange shorts and white tank top.

"What are you staring at?" She asked.

"You have some thing on your lip." He reached over and rubbed at it. "Looks like toothpaste." He licked it from his finger. "Yep toothpaste." She stared at him in disbelief, did he just do that? His touch had made her body tingle, she was aware that her nipples were hard and so was he by the way he stared at her, the lust in his eyes was obvious, he leaned into her and kissed her, she kissed him back.

"You taste like cinnamon." He told her.

"Mouthwash." She said before kissing him again. Her body responded to his touch, she wanted to resist him, her mind said to stop but her heart and her body wanted more.

She pushed him away. "It's getting hot in here." She told him.

"Is something wrong, do you want to stop?"

"No."

"Good, because I don't think I can stop myself." He took her bottom lip between his teeth and sucked on it. Allison shivered with delight.

"Alli-son, I have-to-tell-you—something." He said between kisses.

"What?"

"I'm sorry."

She pulled back from him. "For what?"

"For everything, I've been a jerk, I'm surprised you haven't told me to jump off a bridge yet."

"There have been times, believe me when I wanted to tell you exactly what I thought of you, and forget all about you and this case."

"Not that easy is it?"

"No, I don't know why things are so jumbled I thought maybe Dustin was guilty but then when I saw him I was sure that he is not, and if so, there is a killer still running around."

"We will figure it out, we will, but in the mean time I want you to do something for me."

"What's that?" She asked.

"Make love to me."

She pulled away from him again. "Mr. Lottle what ever gave you the idea that I like you much less want to make love to you." She grinned.

"You were kissing me back."

"Yes, I was."

He scooted closer to her again, stroked her face gently then his hand dropped to her waist, he slid up under her tank top until he found what he was looking for, her breasts were full and firm and her nipples hardened at his touch. "I want you." He whispered in her ear.

"I want you back." She admitted. She stood up pulling him off the couch with her and led him to her bedroom. She pushed him down on the edge of the bed while she stood in front of him, slowly pulling off her top she tossed it to the floor, then she wiggled out of her shorts and panties and stood before him unashamed.

"You are so beautiful." He pulled her to him taking turns at her breasts. Allison's head fell back in satisfaction. He made her want more she wanted more of him, she wanted all of this wonderful man. Her breathing became more rapid as did his, she reached down to feel his erection, it strained against his jeans, she mindlessly pulled at his clothing.

"Help me she begged." Her fingers being clumsy.

He stood and pulled his shirt over his head and they both struggled with the buttons on his pants, finally they gave way sliding to the floor, he kicked them over to the pile where her clothing was.

"I wondered if you were a boxer or brief guy." She snapped the band of his briefs.

"You mean you didn't know?" She thought he was going to go into how she should have known that if she were a real psychic but he didn't. He quickly stepped out of his shorts, she ran her hands over his magnificent body, strong muscles that flexed at her touch, she kissed him along his cheek, his neck and chest, she inched down towards his navel, he shuddered, and thought to himself that he could very easily fall in love with this woman.

He pulled her up off the floor and laid her out on the bed, he explored her body the same way that she had his. The earth shook violently for a few glorious moments and finally as he lay quietly beside her she wondered if she dare say something breaking the silence. He did it for her.

"I'm worried about you."

"Why?" She propped herself up on her elbow to look at him.

"We have talked about this before."

"I know, but I still think that you could be in trouble."

"Don't you think I would know if my life were in danger?"

"Maybe—but then maybe your too close to the situation that it's scrambled your senses."

She rolled her eyes. "You Don't even believe in my senses." She leaned into him pressing her breasts to his chest.

"Yes I do—I didn't at first but I have done my research on you."

"You checked me out? When?"

"When you first came on the case."

"And?"

"And, you checked out-legit."

Allison didn't know weather to be mad or relieved but when he caressed her again she couldn't help but melt back into his arms, she couldn't be mad at him now.

"That's why I'm scared for you."

"I don't understand."

"You haven't been able to use your abilities much lately, there is something blocking you all I can come up with is that you are to closely involved and it's hindering your abilities."

"Do you honestly think I'm in danger?"

"Yes I do."

"Then what do you suggest I do?"

"I don't want you to be alone at any time."

"So are you going to hire a babysitter to watch over me?"

"I was thinking that maybe you could stay at my house for a while— just until we get all this mess figured out."

"Why Can't you move in with me?"

"Seriously?"

"At least I would be more comfortable in my own home."

"I can understand that, are you sure you would be ok with me here?"

"If you honestly think I'm in danger then I would like for you to stay with me, I'll do what ever you think is necessary."

"I think it's necessary that I be with you, do you have a friend you can call?"

"For what?"

"To come over for a few minutes while I go get my things."

"I think I'll be fine until you get back."

"I'd rather you not be alone, at any time."

"I suppose I can call Teresa, she lives close."

"Please tell me her name isn't Teresa Peebles."

"It's Teresa Manton, why?"

"Long story." He shook his head" I'll tell you about it another time, call her now please."

Allison grabbed the phone and asked if Teresa could come over for a few minutes.

"What did she say?" He asked after she hung up the phone.

"She will be right here, go ahead and go, she's only three blocks away."

He struggled getting his pants on.

"How long will you be gone?"

"Not long if I can help it." He pulled his now wrinkled shirt over his head.

"Do you know how to shoot a gun?"

"Yes, it's been a while but I could if I had to."

"I'll leave this here, just in case." He handed her a thirty eight revolver and then took it back to show her where the safety was.

"I don't like guns, but if it makes you feel better—"

"It does. I'll be back as soon as I can, lock the door behind me and only open it for your friend."

"Ok." She wrapped a sheet around her and followed him to the door locking it behind him.

She ran to the phone like a giddy teenager and called Teresa for real this time, she only pretended to call her earlier so Jeremy wouldn't worry.

"Can you and Louisa handle the pet shop a while longer?"

"Yes."

"Jeremy thinks I'm in danger and he wants me to hide out, actually he went to his place To get some clothes, I told him you were on the way here so he wouldn't worry about leaving me alone."

"So I should come over?"

"I'll be fine, He should be back in thirty minutes or so."

"Jeremy? What happened to detective Lottle?"

"Well......."

"Allison, tell me you didn't sleep with the enemy."

"He is not the enemy—anymore."

"So you did sleep with him."

"Maybe."

"I'll be right over, I have to hear this story and you will leave nothing out."

"Ok."

"Give me ten minutes."

"I'll be here."

When Teresa hung up Allison thought she heard another click on the line, she looked down at the receiver still in her hand, was it possible someone had been listening in on her call? Or was it just that Jeremy had her scared?

Seventeen

Allison dressed and sat down in front of the television, Teresa would be there soon and then maybe she wouldn't be so paranoid. She realized that she was tired from the lovemaking and unwillingly dozed off thinking about Jeremy. When the doorbell rang waking her up she didn't think twice before opening the door. There was no one there, She looked out into the yard and saw nothing, Jeremy's warnings rang out through her mind but her curiosity got the best of her, she slowly stepped out onto the porch looking to her left and then to her right, she heard a noise at the back of the house, against her better judgment she followed the noise leaving the front door ajar so she wouldn't lock herself out. There was a rustling in the bushes and she heard a kitten meow, she followed the tiny voice until she found it. A little calico kitten was stuck in the shrubs on the side of the house. "Hello Kitty. What brings you here?"

"Meow." Was her answer.

Allison got on her knees and worked her way into the shrubs stretching until she finally reached the critter and grabbed him by the skin of his neck.

"Your ok, I have you." The kitten was not content he squirmed and wiggled, Allison tried to hold on but she could feel her skin ripping with every swipe the kitten made. Finally she let him go and he ran quickly from the yard.

Jeremy and Teresa pulled up at the same time. She smiled at him oddly.

"What's with you?" He asked, assuming this was Teresa Manton.

"I don't know what you mean."

"Your looking at me funny."

"Maybe I always look this way."

"Is that so?"

"Yeah, why do you look so happy?" She asked him.

"Maybe I always look happy."

"Not from what I hear." Oops, maybe she shouldn't let him know that Allison tells her almost everything that has gone on between them.

"I thought you would have been here sooner, I wanted you here while I was gone."

"Sorry, Allison didn't sound like it was that vital."

"It is to me." Jeremy looked to the front door and his brow furrowed when he realized the front door was ajar.

"What is it?" She asked.

"I don't know but I don't like it." They reached the front door side by side, he grabbed Teresa's arm before she opened the door further. "You stay right here, I'll check it out."

"I want to go with you."

"No, squat down behind this bush and wait for me."

"Be careful." She warned.

He crept up to the door and slowly pushed it open, he had his gun drawn. The living room was empty the television was still on, he moved down the hall to the bedroom, the sheets were still strewn about but he saw no one, he looked under the bed, in the closet, in the bathroom, nothing. He came out of the hallway and saw a figure run out of the kitchen, Teresa let out a scream as the figure flew passed her knocking her on her bottom into the bushes. "Allison." Jeremy called. She didn't stop, Jeremy tried to follow but whoever that was ran very fast, it couldn't have been Allison, even though the hair was the same length and color she wouldn't have run from him. Jeremy went back and helped Teresa up from the ground just as Allison came around the side of the house.

"What happened?" They all asked in unison.

"Why was the door left open and why do you have scratches all over your face and arms?"

"Well I—"

"Didn't I tell you to stay in the house?" He broke her off.

"There was a kitten stuck in the shrubs on the side of the house and I didn't want to get locked out so I left the door open."

"You risked your life for a kitten." He asked.

"I'd hardly call it risking my life, he did scratch me up a bit."

"Some one was in your house." Teresa said.

"Who?"

"We don't know, she was running so fast. She looked like you from behind."

"She was in my house?" Jeremy put his arm around her sensing that she now believed him when he said that she might be in danger. "I'm ok." She told him.

He looked at her wounds closer. "Really, I'm ok." She assured him.

"A kitten." He shook his head.

"Can you honestly tell me that you wouldn't have helped a poor helpless kitten?"

"I think if I were in your situation I can honestly say I would have let the kitten do for itself."

"Amen brother." Teresa added.

"I'm almost ashamed of you two."

"Yeah, whatever." He said. "We can't stay here now." He led her by her elbow inside the house.

"Why not?"

"What if she comes back?"

"She is probably harmless."

"She was in your house."

"Isn't that why you're here? To protect me."

"I think I can better protect you at my house, now get Henry and some things and let's go."

"That's it." She looked to Teresa for back up but her friend seemed to be on the other side, working against her.

"He is right Allison, I think you would be safer at his place.

"All right, you win, I'll get some things packed." She called for Henry when he didn't come she got worried, hopefully he had not slipped out while the door was open. she began to panic, what if he had been taken by the woman that ran from her house? What if that woman was the killer, she couldn't live with herself if anything were to happen to Henry. She went into the bedroom and sat down on the side of the bed, she heard a whimper. She tossed the sheets off the bed and found Henry rolled up in a ball. She picked him up and hugged him. "I was so worried about you." she kissed his precious little face.

"He is going with us right?" Jeremy stood at the door watching her.

"Yes, but when he didn't come after I called him I thought something bad had happened to him."

"He's fine doll face, get your bag packed and let's go."

She held Henry with one hand and tossed things into a bag with the other, when it was full she shoved it into Jeremy's arms. "I'm ready."

"Take care of my friend." Teresa told Jeremy.

"I will." He walked Teresa to her car and saw her off. He ushered Allison and Henry to his car.

"I don't really like the idea of leaving my car here."

"It will be fine."

"I'm not so sure."

"It's a car Allison, if anything happens to it I will personally buy you another one."

"I'm going to hold you to that."

They rode to Jeremy's in silence, she looked out the window into the night not paying much attention to where they were going but when they came to a certain housing addition and he turned into it she perked up.

"Wow, this is a nice neighborhood."

"Yeah, neighbors are friendly enough."

"How do you afford this on a cops salary?" The homes that they drove by were large and well maintained.

"We haven't got to my place yet."

She seemed to be getting excited over nothing, when they pulled up into his driveway the light shown onto a garage that clearly needed painting, the green paint was peeling and flaking off onto the concrete below, window shutters were loose and the flower beds were hideous. He could tell by her silence that she was no longer impressed.

"I told you not to get to excited."

"What happened?" She regretted asking the minute it came out of her mouth.

"I got a great deal on the place, it was a repossession."

"Did it look like this when you bought it?" She put her hand over her mouth.

"It's all right, I know it looks bad, I just haven't had time to work on it. He thought back to new years eve when he sat alone in front of the television set and actually thought about fixing the place up, now he wished that he had, or had at least attempted, but he hadn't lied about not having the time, Allison knew better than any one how many hours he was putting in on this case because she was putting in the same hours.

He finally got out of the car and went around to the other side to help her out, she scooped up Henry and he grabbed her bag. "What have you got in this thing?"

"It's not that heavy."

"Whatever." He opened the front door and reached for a light switch, one of the bulbs went dim and burnt out all together leaving the room dark and full of shadows. She walked inside and set Henry down. He sniffed around the room.

"Don't you dare pee on anything mister." Jeremy warned. Henry gave him a look as if to say he would do anything he darn well pleased.

"Maybe I should take him outside now." It looked as if he had decent enough carpet and she didn't want Henry to ruin it for him.

"Take him out the patio door right there off the kitchen." He pointed.

She turned around the corner and had to catch her breath, the kitchen was beautiful, it was as if she had walked into a different house, the cabinets looked brand new and the counters were green granite, the floor had new wood planks.

"Wow!."

"I told you it wasn't all bad."

"It's great, I love it."

"Do you like to cook?" He asked her.

"I don't do much cooking but I wouldn't mind learning in a kitchen like this." She admitted.

"Put Henry out and let him do his business, he will be fine by himself, the yard is fenced, he can't go anywhere." She reluctantly let Henry out and shut the door behind him.

"Are you hungry?"

"Yes, I am."

"Sit down, I'll make us something quick."

She pulled up a barstool and sat at the counter while he rummaged through the stainless steel refrigerator and set out some bacon, eggs and shredded cheese. He put the bacon on to fry and cracked the eggs in a cup mixing in salt pepper and a dab of milk.

"You look like you have done this before."She told him.

"All the time."

"So, a lot of women pass through this kitchen huh?"

"No, I do cook for myself though."

"So there hasn't been a lot of women through here?"

"Nosey body." He accused.

"I'm just curious."

"Yes, you are." He kissed her on the forehead before pouring the egg mixture into the skillet.

"There must have been some women if you don't want to talk about it."

He firmly put the spatula down and turned to look directly at her. "Yes Allison there have been many women in my life, but none of them have made me as crazy as you do."

"Thank you, I think." She pondered a moment. " Crazy how? Pull your hair out crazy? Loosing your ever lovin mind crazy? Pull a gun out and shoot some one crazy?"

He put his hands on her either side of her face and held it there so that she could not look away from him. "You make me want to wake up in the morning, you make me want to sleep at night so I can dream about you and every time I see you I want to do this." He kissed her long and hard and by the time he released her she was dizzy and breathless.

"That's the kind of crazy you make me."

"I like that kind of crazy."

There was a scratching at the glass door. "I almost forgot about Henry." She jumped off the stool the heel of her shoe catching on the pedestal and before she knew what was happening she was on the floor with Jeremy standing over her, she could tell he wanted to laugh but he didn't. "Are you all right doll face?"

He held his hand out to help her up. Henry continued to scratch and bark. Jeremy lifted her into his arms and carried her to the couch. "Are you hurt?"

"Just my ego, what a klutz."

"It happens, matter of fact I fell in the exact same spot just yesterday."

"Liar."

"Would it make you feel better if it were true?"

"No."

"Ok, I didn't really fall. But I could have."

"I better let Henry in before he tears the door down. Thanks anyway for trying to make me feel less like a moron."

"I'm kind of partial to moron's."

She swatted at him. "I'd do just about anything for you Allison Kramer."

"I feel the same about you Jeremy." He kissed her again, each kiss was better than the last.

"That was nice, I hear ringing." She told him.

"Crap, my food is burning." He ran into the kitchen with her on his heels he ran to the stove while she fanned a towel at the smoke detector trying to get it to stop it's annoying beeping.

"I hope you like your bacon well done."

"I'm sorry." She told him. Knowing that it was her clumsiness that made him forget about the food on the stove.

Henry was really barking up a storm now. She ran to the door and let him in.

He raced to the kitchen with his nose in the air.

"It's your mama's fault boy."

"Wait a minute." She protested.

"I'm just kidding, I take full responsibility for ruining our dinner."

"It's ok, I'm not real hungry anymore." She looked at him seductively. He felt the sudden need to adjust himself. " Oh forget this." He said tossing the scorched skillet into the sink, he scooped her into his arms again.

"Where are you taking me"

"To my bed, where I am going to show you just how crazy I am about you."

"I like the sound of that."

They retreated down the hall leaving Henry in the kitchen with a few slices of well done bacon to keep him occupied. He Didn't seem to mind.

Eighteen

Dalana lay beside her young officer, she loved him so much he had saved her life when her father had left her for dead that day nearly two years ago. He looked directly in her eyes before the car burst into flames her seatbelt was stuck, she struggled to get it released while he helped her sister out of the car, Dustin managed to get himself out but none of them had come back to help her, she never blamed her mother, Vanessa had always tried to bring peace to the family but it never seemed to work, and she would admit that a lot of it was her fault but not all of it. Dalana thought back to that fateful day, as the flames licked around the car threatening to burn her alive, she finally managed to get her seat belt undone and roll out the passenger side door right as the car exploded into a fireball, not knowing the car had stopped beside a steep embankment she rolled time after time until finally her body came to a stop, she knew she wasn't dead but she couldn't move or speak. The last thing she heard was sirens, and her mother screaming for her. And then there was darkness and silence. When she woke up Bobby Sampson was beside her, holding her hand. "Do you know who you are, where you are?" He asked her. At the time she was in so much pain and she could not remember much, her entire body seemed to be wrapped in gauze.

Bobby knew who she was, he had lived a few blocks from the Gamble family, he had driven by the house when the girls were outside doing cheerleading practice, Dalana wasn't into it much, He could tell, to most people the girls looked identical but he could tell the difference, Destiny was shallow, Dalana was deep, she had a look in her eyes, like she had lived well beyond her years, there was still something she hid from him, hid from the world and one day he would figure it out and then he would know why the girl he loved was so sad. Bobby had found Dalana at the bottom of that hill and taken her to a hospital out of town as a Jane Doe, he assumed responsibility for her which wasn't hard him being an officer of the law, no one questioned him, he took vacation time to care for her day and night, he saw her through several plastic surgeries, her face looked just as it had before the accident but her body was left scarred and bruised from all the skin Grafts.

"What are we going to do?" She asked Bobby.

"About what?"

"You know what I'm talking about Bobby, when everyone realizes that I am alive and that—"No one knows your alive so don't worry about it."

"I am worried about it, My mother saw me, my brother saw me. He is terrified of me."

"Of course he is, he thinks your dead. I told you to stay away from that place it would only bring trouble and now you have, you've—"

"What Bobby? What have I done?"

"You've killed your mother and made your brother worse off than he was."

"I can't believe you think I killed my mother Bobby." She was shocked that he would think her a killer. She could be mean but she could never kill.

"Can you blame me for thinking that way? You harbored such ill feeling towards your entire family, your brother never physically hurt anyone before so I don't think he killed her, or anyone else"

"But you think I did? Your supposed to love me Bobby."

"I do love you Dalana but look at it from my side for a second, some one is killing people that have been in someway linked to you and they are leaving bits of red velvet at the scenes, I now find out that you have been sneaking out of the house at night. I don't know where you have been going other than to see your mother and brother, how could I not be a little suspicious?"

"I didn't kill my mother, I had no reason to, sure I was mad at her for not taking up for me, for not seeing how rotten my father treated me, and Dustin. Something happened with Dustin Bobby. I don't know what but he wasn't always like he is now, he wasn't born that way."

"What are you suggesting?"

"I don't know but I think it's something my father did. I have to find out the truth."

He had clearly upset her to the point of tears and she kept rattling on about something that had happened in the past, he was determined to find out what Mr. Gamble had done to destroy his family.

"No more secrets Dalana, tell me what your hiding. Tell me what you didn't tell your mother."

Dalana hesitated before finally starting to talk. "He climbed into my bed one night-"What the hell did he do?"

"He thought I was Destiny, he put his hand over my mouth to keep me from calling out." She stopped talking.

"Please Dalana, tell me. When you woke up after the accident you begged me not to tell your family that you were alive. I knew right then that something terrible had happened for you to rather them believe you were dead than go home. Did he rape you?"

"No, but he would have. He was drunk and passed out before he could."

"Thank God."

"But in the morning everything changed, he couldn't look me in the eye. He hated me for what he wanted to do, I think he hated me more because I hadn't been Destiny, he always loved her but now I know that it was a sick kind of love and—"

"And what? Is there more?"

"A few weeks later when he thought we were all away for the night, except for Dustin I had snuck into the house to get something I had forgotten and I saw Dustin run out of his bedroom crying, he did something horrible to that boy that night. I can't prove it but that is the night that Dustin went into a shell and I don't know if he will ever come out of it."

"I'll kill him, I'll kill that bastard for whatever he has done to you and your family."

"I hated Destiny for years because he loved her more than me but I should have pitied her for the kind of love he felt for her."

"We have to tell some one about this."

"We can't, you can't tell anyone cause then we have to tell them I'm alive. I'm scared."

"There is nothing to be scared of Dalana."

"He let me die for a reason, what if he finds out I'm alive and tries to kill me for real this time."

"I won't let him, I will protect you."

"I know you will try but—"

"Ok, for now I won't say anything. But this won't stay hidden forever Dalana."

"Thank you Bobby."

"I love you D."

"I love you too." She fell back into his arms where she felt safe.

"Do you think he killed my mom? My dad that is?"

"Maybe, but I don't know why anyone would kill your mom."

"She talked to me when I went there that night."

"You were there the night she was killed? My God Dalana who saw you?"

"The staff thought I was Destiny, they let me walk right in. I stopped to see Dustin, he was asleep and then I went to see mom. She knew who I was the second she saw me. People always got us mixed up but mom always knew who we were even when we were very young and tried to fool her she was never fooled she could always tell us apart."

"She talked to you?"

"She said she was sorry about the car accident, she said she loved me. I think she thought I was a ghost."

"What else was she sorry about?""

"Are you implying that she knew my Dad was a pervert and chose to ignore it?"

"Maybe."

No, she loved us more than anything including him, if she thought he was hurting us she would have taken us and ran. I don't know who would have killed her Bobby."

"Detective Lottle has a psychic working with him so maybe they can get the answers for us. I've been nosy but I haven't learned much except that he thinks your brother is the killer."

172

"He wouldn't, he couldn't kill anyone."

"They found him holding evidence that put him at a murder scene."

"So, you said they found him standing over mom with the bloody knife in his hand and I still don't believe he did it. Some one is setting him up."

"I think your right D."

*

Jeremy snored loudly, he was getting the best sleep he had gotten in a long time maybe he was just so physically tired from making love to Allison, or maybe he was just mentally exhausted from this case. Whatever it was he needed the rest and he was getting it now.

Allison was still nestled in the crook of his arm. Henry had come in at some point and jumped up on the bed with them, he was now at the foot of the bed between their feet. Allison grew restless and tiptoed into the kitchen, she jumped as a tree branch rustled up against one of the windows, suddenly feeling chilled she grabbed a quilt off of the couch and wrapped it around her shoulders. She opened the refrigerator and stuck her head inside.

"Pizza."

"I wouldn't eat that if I were you."

She jumped banging her head on the refrigerator shelf. "Ouch!."

"Didn't mean to scare you sweet thing." He wrapped his arms around her waist.

"I couldn't sleep."

"So you decided to raid the fridge?"

"I hope you don't mind."

"No, but I still wouldn't touch the pizza, it's been there a while."

"Ok, pizza is out, what else have you got in here?" She poked her head back in the fridge and rummaged around."

"Pancakes." He said.

"I love pancakes."

"Then I'll make some." He noticed that she was shivering. "Why Don't you go on and get a nice hot shower and when you get back your breakfast will be waiting."

"I was hoping to have your company in the shower." She raised her eyebrows, and slid the quilt off her shoulders in an effort to seduce him.

"There will be plenty of time for that I promise."

"I knew it."

"You knew what?"

"You Can't keep up with me."

"Oh please, I assure you that is not the case."

"Right."

Jeremy kept mixing the batter until it was to it's desired consistency. "Your running out of time, better get moving." He patted her on the fanny and steered her out of the kitchen.

Allison stood under the spray of the hot water, washing away reminders of the night before, but there was no sadness because she was sure that there were plenty more nights with Jeremy in the future, she had fallen hard for the great detective Lottle.

"Pancakes are ready." She heard him yell from the hallway. She quickly dried off and pulled one of his t-shirts over her head. She then wrapped the towel on her head like a turban and pranced down the hallway to the dining table where Jeremy was already seated. There were pancakes and strawberries and three flavors of syrup.

"Wow! It all looks so good."

"So do you."

"No sir mister, you had your chance. All I want now is food."

She pulled out a chair and sat down across from him, he couldn't take his eyes off of her.

"Is something wrong?"

"No."

"Then why are you staring at me?"

"Because your beautiful." She blushed.

"Stop it."

"Well you are."

"Thank you Jeremy."

"Don't thank me, thank your mama she must be beautiful too."

"She is."

"I'd like to meet her sometime."

"When?"

"When ever your ready." He took a bite of his pancake. " Go ahead and eat before it gets cold."

"She took a bite and then another. "This is a damn good pancake." Henry whined looking up at her. Allison tore off a piece and handed it to him under the table.

"Why do you want to meet my mom?"

"Because I want to know more about you, your family."

"All you have to do is ask me."

"I want to meet your family is that so bad?"

Allison's heart skipped a beat she knew that her mother would like him, she wasn't sure if her father would like any man that she brought home, she was his little girl and as far as he was concerned no one was good enough for her. She was positive her younger sister would like him, Probably too much. "Maybe when we get this case solved we can go see my family."

"Have you told them about me?"

"Should I have told them about you?"

He looked upset. She wondered if she should tell him that she had told her mother about him. She decided against it. Let him wonder a while longer. She gobbled down the rest of the pancake and chased it down with a glass of milk.

"What are we doing today?" She asked.

"I was thinking that we might go see Destiny Gamble and hopefully get inside her house, you seem to think she would let us look around."

"I don't think she's hiding anything, so therefore she would have no reason not to let us in."

"So then let's pay her a visit."

"I'm in."

"Ruff Ruff." Henry added.

"I think you better stay here baby boy."

"Why Can't he go with us?

"Really?"

"Sure, it's not hot outside, he will be fine in the car, we'll crack the windows."

"If your sure."

"I'm sure, get dressed we have work to get done."

Nineteen

Destiny squinted as the sun peeked in from the window blinds, she rolled over in bed to face the wall that showcased photos of her family, when the family had been happy. She hadn't realized before how many pictures had been taken that her father had been absent from, sometimes things weren't always as they appeared to be. Her mothers image smiled at her, she smiled back, she missed her mom, she missed her sister, even though they weren't close when she died she missed her. She missed the boy that her brother had once been. The phone rang bringing her out of her nostalgia.

"Hello."

She was surprised to hear detective Lottle's voice asking if he could come to her house to talk and look around. "Sure, that would be fine—no I am not going back to school, I am going to continuation school now. I'll be here." Destiny had no idea what this visit was about but she hoped that it didn't mean bad news for her brother. Detective Lottle hadn't kept it a secret that he thought Dustin was guilty of the murders but it was just as clear that his partner Miss Kramer thought he was innocent, and Destiny was counting on her to prove it. She rolled out of her bed and pulled the blanket up making it look halfway made up. The rest of the house was virtually spotless so what if she skimped on her bed making this morning. Since she had decided not to go back to school she had cleaned the house constantly. She had also had a lot of time to reflect on her life and she had decided that making cheerleading her main focus in life had been time wasted, she could have spent more time with her family, she could have done more good deeds to help the less fortunate. If she could only turn back time she would have done many things differently. She wouldn't have spent so much time fighting with her sister and maybe they could have even been best friends as well as sisters. She had known about her fathers affairs but she chose to keep them from her mother maybe she should have told her about them.

Destiny soaked in her bubble bath with her eyes closed remembering a time when the triplets were young and happy playing in the sprinkler in the front yard, she could almost hear the laughing as if it were actually happening right then. Dustin was such a happy child, normal. No one could ever explain what had caused his mental breakdown but things started to change around the time they turned eight and by the time they turned sixteen, a few months before Dalana's death it worsened. She wiped the tears from her face, it did no one any good to cry about it now, she had wasted a lot of time in the tub and the detectives would be there soon. She pulled a towel off the rack and suddenly she froze, her breath caught in her throat. Her father was standing in the door way, she thought she had locked that door.

"What are you doing in here?"

"I'm sorry, I thought I heard you crying."

"I'm fine."

He just stared at her making no attempt to leave the room. He reached out and caressed her bare shoulder. She didn't like the way it made her feel.

"I said I'm fine, you can leave now."

She pulled away from him.

"I'm going to work—I'm sorry." He turned and left the room but Destiny stayed put until she heard the front door slam.

Jeremy and Allison pulled up to the curb just as Mr. Gamble was backing his corvette out of the driveway.

"He seems to be in a hurry."

"Yes, and I have an uneasy feeling about it." She told him.

The corvette peeled out, squealing its tires on the pavement seemingly trying to make a quick escape.

Allison didn't wait for Jeremy she jumped out of the explorer and sprinted for the front door of the Gamble house ringing the bell several times before Destiny finally answered.

"What happened?" Allison asked.

"Nothing."

"Are you sure? Your father seemed to be in a big hurry to get out of here, and you look upset."

"We just had a disagreement, that's all."

"Are you sure that your all right?"

"Allison, don't pressure the girl, if she say's that she is fine let her be." Jeremy warned.

He didn't want her scared or spooked or anything that might make here change her mind about letting them look through the house, because somewhere in that house lay some answers to this case.

Destiny stood aside so that they could enter the house. "It was just a disagreement, it wasn't our first and I know it won't be our last. Come on in."

She closed the door behind them, shivering from the cold January air. It was hard to believe that a new year was beginning and this year might prove to be a worse year than the previous two she had struggled through.

"I don't know what your looking for Detective but if it means that you can prove my brother is innocent then you have my permission to tear this house apart for all I care."

"I wouldn't go that far Miss Gamble."

"I'll be in the kitchen, I have some homework to do, my brothers room is here, aside from dusting and vacuuming I haven't touched anything since he moved into the home. Dalana's room is there." She pointed down the hallway. "It hasn't been touched either, since her death. I never go in my Dads room but feel free to look in there as well... I'll leave you two to look for whatever your looking for."

"Thank you Destiny."

"Sure." She walked off leaving Allison and Jeremy standing in the long hall wondering where to start their search. Allison was drawn to Dustin's room. Jeremy followed her, she seemed to be on a mission, maybe her so called vibes were back, they walked into the boys room, the walls were covered with racing memorabilia, posters of NASCAR drivers."

"Wow! I might have liked this kid, if he weren't a suspect." Jeremy said.

"I still like him." Allison admitted.

"I know you do, and to be honest that scares me."

Allison ran her hand across the dresser that had been recently dusted, just like Destiny had said. She watched as Jeremy rummaged through the boys closet, there were baseballs and uniforms, footballs. "It looks like the frail, timid boy we know wasn't always that way." Jeremy turned to see Allison looking through a photo album, she held it up so that Jeremy could see Pictures of Dustin in his ball uniforms. "Not only did he like sports, he played them." Jeremy wanted to kick himself for feeling sorry for the boy, he was after all a potential killer and he absolutely refused to let his guard down when it came to Dustin Gamble.

"Something bad happened to Dustin in this house." Allison said, but for some reason he is blocking me.

"Who is blocking you?"

"Dustin, he doesn't want any one to know, he is ashamed. She closed the photo album and stood up. "Let's go to Dalana's room." Jeremy followed her down the hall, her room was as clean as her brothers considering she had been dead for two years, her closet held cheerleader pompoms even though she hadn't been nearly as interested in cheerleading as her sister had been.

"I feel weird combing through a teen aged girls belongings." Jeremy admitted.

"Well if it bothers you that much just stand over there while I do it."

"Fine." He leaned against the wall while Allison lifted up the mattress on the bed.

"What are you doing?" He asked.

"Looking for her diary."

"How do know she even kept a diary?"

"I was a teen age girl once, believe me she had a diary." She felt around under the mattress and feeling something, she pulled it out and held it up, a small pink book with diary spelled out in glittery gold letters.

"I told you she would have one." She told him, waving it in his face.

"It has a lock on it, so miss know it all where is the key?"

"Come on, it shouldn't be too hard to break this little lock." She twisted and pulled but the lock remained tight.

"Maybe I'll look around for a key." He suggested.

Allison had become so frustrated that she needed a time out she sat on the bed holding the book on her lap, she closed her eyes and when she did Dalana was in her mind. She was in that very room but she was not alone, some one was with her, as she slept he watched her. The man whispered but Allison could not make out what he said. The man undressed and slid into bed with the sleeping girl. She woke up and started to scream but a hand went over her mouth. Allison opened her eyes, she didn't want to see what she was sure had happened next. "I think Dalana was molested."

"By who?"

"I'm not sure, maybe her father."

"No way, that's sick—why would he do that to his own child?"

"Why would any one, but you know it happens Jeremy, you're the cop you have seen what people are capable of."

"That's true."

"I'm not positive it was him but I just saw a vision of a man crawling naked into bed with Dalana, and he put his hand over her mouth to keep her quiet.

"Wouldn't she have told someone about it if he had done that?"

"Not if she were scared, he could have threatened to hurt her, or her siblings."

"He could have let her die in that crash to keep her quiet about that." Jeremy said.

"Now your thinking like a true Detective again."

"Yeah, maybe you can make it your new gig as well."

"Seriously, I think after this case is out of the way I'll go back to the pet shop and be happy again."

"So your not happy working with me?"

"Don't twist my words Mr. Lottle"

"So you will miss me?"

"Yes I will miss you." A few short weeks ago she never thought she would feel that way about him, but it would be sad when the case was solved and she would go back to her life and not see him every day. She found herself saddened by the thought.

Jeremy spotted something shiny on the floor barely peeking out from under the bed, he thought it might be the diary key. It was a key.

"Give me that." She said ripping it from his hand. Allison fumbled with the lock but there was no way around it, it wasn't the right key.

"Damn it." She cursed hurling the book across the room. It hit the wall and landed with a thud on the floor. Jeremy picked it up. "Good news, it's open." They sat on the bed and read the first half of the book together, it gave them little information, at first. Mostly about girlfriends and the arguments they'd had. Jeremy got bored with it and searched the room some more while Allison continued reading. He was in the closet when he came across a red velvet coat, it was nice not to mention very similar to the red velvet that had been found with all of the victims

"Check this out." He held it up for Allison to see.

"Is that Velvet?"

"Yes it is."

"Listen to this." She began to read from the diary. "That strange boy drove by the house again today, he looked directly into my eyes, we connected on some level, I think he lives nearby, he looks a few years older than me. I'd like to meet him."

"Well, I wonder who he is?

"I don't know, maybe there is more about him." Allison kept reading, and Jeremy kept snooping.

"I'm going to look in the old man's room."

"Ok." She said with out looking up from the diary.

Jeremy could hear Destiny in another part of the house, she was still typing away on her laptop, he was surprised that she hadn't come to check on them, most people would not have allowed them to search so freely through personal belongings. He turned the knob to the parents bedroom door, it was locked. Mr. Gamble hadn't known about them coming to look around so why would he lock the door?

"Destiny." He stood over her shoulder.

"You scared me."

"I apologize, would it be possible to take a look in your parents bedroom?"

"Sure, I told you it was fine."

"It seems to be locked."

"Really?" Her brow furrowed. "I wonder when he started locking the door."

"I guess that means you don't have a key."

"No, but I can get in anyway."

Jeremy followed her down the hall, he watched while she picked at the lock with a nail file and in no time she had the door open.

"Thanks." He was impressed.

"Your welcome, but if anyone asks the door was unlocked."

"Trust me, your secret is safe with me." He assured her.

Destiny stared at the floor.

"Is there something wrong?"

"My Dad has been acting real strange lately, he has been for years actually but more so lately."

"Since Dalana died?"

"Actually it started before she died, he won't talk about it though. All he seems to be interested in are women and cars."

"Sounds like a midlife crisis or something." He Didn't know what to tell her.

"Something is not right with him."

Jeremy picked up a picture off of the dresser, the whole Gamble family was in it but none of them were smiling.

"That was taken the day of the crash."

"Is that velvet Dalana is wearing?"

"Yes. Her velvet skirt and coat, her favorite, of course it was too hot that day to be wearing it, She wore the skirt anyway, the coat it still in her closet."

"She loved red and she loved the feel of velvet on her skin, she said."

"Interesting."

"If you say so, I really need to get back to my school work."

"Yes, I'm sorry to keep you."

Destiny walked back down the hall almost running into Allison as she came out of Dalana's room.

"Excuse me Destiny."

"It's ok."

Allison rushed into the parents room.

"Where's the fire?" Jeremy asked.

"Dalana is not dead."

He hadn't expected to hear that. "What do you mean she isn't dead?

"I can't explain it, I just feel it, she isn't dead."

"So do you think she is our killer trying to frame her brother?"

"I don't think she is our killer but I do think her brother is being framed by some one."

"Don't forget the red velvet, how does that figure in? It is Dalana's favorite material."

"That doesn't mean she is a killer and her liking red velvet is more reason that it wouldn't be her. why would she leave something at crime scenes that would implicate her?"

"Yeah I know it makes no sense."

"Unless she did and wanted us to know it's her, maybe she wants us to know that she is alive."

"She may want us to know she is alive but she is no killer."

"We are jumping the gun anyway, we have no proof that she is still alive."

"No not yet, but listen to this excerpt—I saw BS today, yes I now know who he is, he was shocked to see me, he lives two blocks from us—"

"Is BS his initials or is she abbreviating for bull shit?" He grinned.

"Ha-ha, very funny, shut your trap and listen to the rest of this."

"Yes Mam."

"He was washing his truck, he is so tall and handsome and he looks really good in his uniform—"

Jeremy waited but she never said anything else.

"Is that it?"

"That's it, it's like she got interrupted before she could finish the paragraph. But listen, she talked about this BS guy in uniform, you know I've had an uneasy feeling about officer Sampson."

"It would explain why he is so interested in this case, why he pops up everywhere that we are."

"What if he is our killer? What if he is doing this to avenge his girlfriends death."

"If he were avenging his girlfriend then why wouldn't he target people that supposedly did her wrong her," He asked.

"Hello, Vanessa Gamble was stabbed to death." She reminded him.

"I remember very well."

"This is my theory. Somehow Dalana survived that terrible crash and officer Sampson found her, saved her, and for some reason is keeping her hidden." She said.

"Maybe she wants to stay hidden, maybe she wants to stay dead to the world."

"What if Allison—what if he is holding her against her will—Robert."

"Who is Robert?" She asked.

"Robert Sampson AKA Bobby. We will check him out as soon as we leave here." He promised.

"Ok, what are we looking for in Dad's room?" She asked.

"Anything out of place, Destiny said that he has been acting like a different person since before Dalana died and I want to know why, I want to know what would make a man completely change and alienate his family." He found he might as well have been talking to himself because Allison had gone back to the diary, she was enthralled once again.

Mr. Gamble seemed to have and entire entertainment system in his bedroom, thirty two inch television, video cassette recorder DVD player/ recorder, a video camera still set up in the corner of the room, Jeremy looked to see if there was a tape in it, there wasn't.

"Oh my goodness." Allison said from the corner of the room, where she had been leaning against the wall. She slid down the wall to land on the floor with a thud.

"What is it?"

"Dalana says that one night when Destiny was sleeping over at a friends house her father came in drunk and climbed into bed with her—that's the vision I saw earlier."

"Maybe it was an accident."

"She writes that when she protested he covered her mouth and planted kisses all over her face, he called her Destiny. Apparently he passed out before anything else could happen."

"Thank God. I'm telling you Allison this man is hiding something more than that night. And I think it's in this room."

"What could be worse than what I'm reading? The man crawled into bed with his daughter, it doesn't matter that he thought it was Destiny, it still would have been a daughter, that is so sick." She continued to read. It appeared Mr. Gamble was a collector of DVD's and video tapes, in his closet Jeremy found a glass case full of them but of course it was locked.

"Maybe Destiny can pick that lock too." Allison suggested.

"We won't need her too."

"Why not?"

"With what we can see in this room and what you have in that diary we should have enough to get a search warrant for that case."

"Listen to this, Three weeks after that night Mom was out of town and we were supposed to be staying with friends except for Dustin, he was home with Dad, I came back to get something from my room, no one knew I was home, I saw Dustin come out of their bedroom, he was crying and very upset. I don't know what happened that night but it messed that boy up good."

"Great, now he's molesting the boy too."

"We don't know that for sure."

"Allison, do you think Mr. Gamble read that diary?"

"I don't know, why?"

"It would give him reason for letting her parish in that crash."

"He would have also destroyed the evidence." She told him.

"Crap, I'm so off my game it's not funny." Jeremy ran his hands through his hair.

"Why is that Jeremy?"

"I blame you Allison Kramer, you have thrown me for a loop and I cant think straight."

He kissed her on the tip of her nose.

"What do you suppose is on all of those disks?" She asked him.

"I don't want to know, it can't be good."

"We should get out of here, Gamble is on his way home." She told him.

"Are you sure?"

"I'm positive." They carefully put everything back in it's place and locked the door behind them.

"Destiny, thank you so much for your help, we will have to come back but please for now do not tell your Dad that we were here."

"You found something didn't you?"

"We found your sisters diary that suggests some things about your father, but we need a search warrant to get into your Dad's locked case."

"What case?"

"The one in his closet"

Jeremy wished Allison would keep her trap shut for once, she could be blowing the Whole case by telling Destiny this. For all he knew Destiny was setting this whole thing up, she could be the killer. At this point anything was possible. After all it was a strange thing for her to let a cop in to search freely through the house.

"I won't tell him that you were here, he would be furious with me."

"Thank you Destiny, are you going to be ok?"

"Why wouldn't I be?"

"I just want to be sure your ok."

"I'll be just fine when you find the killer and put my brother back at Rustling Winds."

"I want him out of that horrible place just as much as you do Destiny. I promise I will do my best."

"Let's go." Jeremy pulled her out the door and rushed her to the car. Henry was still in the same spot on the backseat right where he was when they had gotten there, however he was obviously happy that they had returned.

"Sometimes you just say too much." He told her as they pulled away from the Gamble house.

"What did I say now that was so wrong?"

"We still don't know who's guilty and who isn't, that girl could be involved somehow and your talking to her and treating her as if she were completely innocent."

"Are you saying she isn't?"

"I'm saying that at this point in the game everyone is still very much a suspect and should be treated as such. Allison sat on her side of the car and silently pouted, maybe he was right, there was a possibility as slight as it was that Destiny could be guilty of something. Even Dustin. But her gut said no, her gut instinct told her that they were both victims in this mess. Dalana however was still in question. Jeremy wanted to say something to her but he decided he would be better off to keep his mouth shut, as they rounded the block they passed Tom Gambles' blue corvette.

"Tom." She said.

"Yep, there he is, you were right he almost caught us in his house."

"Tom." She said again.

"I know the mans name Allison."

"The same name as the man who wrote those e mails to Stacy and Jill."

"Surely not the same Tom......you think?"

"Maybe."

"Is this just a guess or are you sure it's the same Tom?"

"I'm not sure, but I know that he is involved some how with the deaths of those girls, I got goose bumps when he drove by."

"Maybe the goose bumps were because we were so close to getting caught in his house."

"No, it's because that man has evil in him."

Jeremy pulled out his cell phone and called captain Johnson

"Tell me some good news Lottle."

"We need a search warrant for Tom Gambles house and car."

"Why?"

"Trust me Cap, this man is hiding something."

"What makes you think so?"

"We just left his house, his daughter let us look around and we found some things that indicate he could be involved in questionable activity."

"You think he is our killer?"

"He's is up to something, it may not be murder but it can't be good."

"Bring me something that will prove to the judge you deserve a warrant."

"I'm bringing it, be there in a few."

"What did you find in that house?"

"His dead daughters diary with some disturbing info in it and a locked up cabinet of DVD's."

"What do you think are on them?"

"Gamble might be a child predator."

"Are you serious."

"Yes, and Allison is sure that Dalana Gamble is alive and well."

"Anything else you want to throw at me?"

"Yes, your new recruit—Sampson."

"What about him?"

"Where is he?"

"He took a few days off, not feeling well he told Phyllis."

"I think you better take some back up and pay him a visit, I believe that's where you will find Dalana Gamble."

"Shoot Lottle, you had nothing two days ago and now your gonna pile it all up on me."

"Sorry, is there any way you can get a head start on that warrant? We are about fifteen minutes away."

"You know the judge is gonna want to see that diary before he issues a warrant and I hope you had permission to take it out of the house."

"Destiny will attest to it, she willingly let us search the house and take the diary."

"I'll see what I can get going."

"Thanks cap."

Red light." Allison yelled. Jeremy slammed on the brakes.

"I hate when people drive and talk on the cell phone."

"Sorry, it had to be done."

"Yeah, you cops think the rules don't apply to you." She chuckled.

"Still cracking jokes at a time like this, just one more thing I like about you Allison Kramer." She leaned over and kissed his cheek. Henry popped up from the backseat licking them both on the face.

"Thanks buddy."

They pulled up to the station and Jeremy carried the diary inside while Allison walked Henry outside giving him a much needed bathroom break.

"Lottle." Captain called form his office when he saw Jeremy walk in.

"Close the door please."

"What's wrong Cap?"

"What makes you think anything is wrong?"

"You don't usually tell me to close the door unless there is a problem."

"I just don't think it's any ones business what goes on with Sampson."

"But we need some one to go get him, therefore someone is going to know something."

"I called Sampson myself?"

"Why? I told you to get back up and go to him, he's probably running right now."

"He's bringing her in."

"What?"

"I told him that we know Dalana is alive and that he needed to bring her in and tell us what they know."

"He Didn't deny it?"

"No, He said that he would bring her in immediately."

"Well, where is he?" He looked around.

"It's only been ten minutes."

'That could very well be a ten minute head start that they have, your just like Allison."

"What do you mean by that remark?"

"Your too trusting."

"Maybe you just don't trust enough Lottle."

He pointed to the door and Jeremy turned to see officer Bobby Sampson, Allison and the girl who had to be Dalana Gamble walking towards them. Phyllis took Henry from Allison as they entered the office.

Jeremy knew that Allison said Dalana was alive but seeing her in person was still a shock, he really should stop doubting the woman so much, so far everything she had envisioned had been true.

"Sampson." Jeremy said acknowledging the younger man." Why Don't you introduce us to your lady friend."

"I'm sure you already know that she is Dalana Gamble."

"We assumed, we have a lot of questions for you young lady."

"I was afraid of that."

"Just answer truthfully and you won't have anything to worry about."

"You Don't have to be afraid of us Dalana, any of us." Allison told her.

"Thank you Ms. Kramer. She said nervously.

"We found your diary Dalana. We have some questions about things you wrote in it."

Dalana looked at her young officer, he took her hand and gave it a reassuring squeeze.

"I think we already know who BS is." He looked at Bobby.

"He is the man that saved my life, if he hadn't picked me up off the side of the road I would surely be dead."

"Why did you let everyone believe you were dead? Why would you put your family through that kind of pain?"

"You weren't there Detective, I was in that car crash, fighting to get out as I watched my Dad come back for my sister and Dustin managed to crawl out, he helped him the other side of the road and instead of coming to help me he just watched me struggle, he watched as the flames burned my skin, he watched as the car blew up, he had time to help me but he didn't, he wanted me dead, why would I be stupid enough to let him know that I wasn't? What if he decided to finish the job for real."

"How did you escape that explosion Dalana?"

"When the car burst into flames I could barely see the outline of my family across the road, I wrestled with the belt until it finally gave, when I opened the door I didn't realize the wreck had spun the car to the edge of a cliff and I fell—I rolled down the steep hill, landing beside another road. I heard the explosion and then I passed out."

"So how did you find her Bobby?"

"I was off duty that night but I listened to the scanner and when I heard the description of the car I knew it belonged to the Gamble family, I headed up the canyon road, I almost didn't see her laying in the ditch because I was looking up at the flames. She was hurt so bad, I begged her to wake up and when she opened her eyes she begged me not to tell any one that she was alive, but she asked me to save her."

"And you did."

"I heard the sirens coming so I carefully carried her to my truck, I drove her all the way to Fresno hospital."

"But she needed help immediately, why didn't you flag down the ambulance?" Captain Johnson asked.

"Because he loves her and would do anything she asked." Allison chimed in.

"Would you kill for her?" Jeremy asked.

"Detective, I admit I have done some questionable things but murder was not one, I've killed no one and neither has Dalana."

"But she did sneak into her mothers room the night she was killed didn't you Dalana?"

"Yes, but I just wanted to see her and Dustin."

'They both knew it was you didn't they?"

"The employees thought I was Destiny and they let me walk on by, but mom and Dustin knew the truth. I went to my brothers room first, he was asleep, I watched him for the longest time, he looked so young and so sweet, I felt guilty for being mean to the boy when we were younger, I treated him badly."

"We know that he is afraid of you."

"I was stupid and mean and jealous of him and Destiny because my Dad loved them more, I was lucky and didn't know it at the time, I didn't need his kind of love."

"What do you mean by that?" Asked Johnson.

"I mean that my dad has secrets, he is hiding more than you think, if you have read my diary then you know what I think is going on."

"We have read it and we are working on a search warrant for your Dad's house."

"Good."

"I'd like to go back to the night of the crash, Bobby picked you up and—"

"I drove her to Fresno, being a cop it was easy enough to show my badge and tell them that she was a Jane Doe in a bad accident and that until we found out her identity I would be responsible for her welfare."

"How badly were you hurt?"

"I had burns, mostly on my stomach and back, cracked ribs, a broken arm. Lots of skin grafts, my face was messed up but not badly enough to leave more than this tiny scar over my eyebrow." She moved her hair aside so that they could see the tiny crescent shape scar.

"She was in the hospital for two months, I took a leave of absence and stayed by her side."

"I couldn't let them know I was alive Detective, if you had seen the look in Dad's eyes you would understand why I thought I was in danger."

"I believe you felt your life was in danger but why would he want you dead?"

"Because I was onto him, that night he stumbled into my room, drunk, pawing at me thinking I was Destiny, he passed out quickly but if he hadn't I know what he would have done to me."

"Why didn't you tell some one what happened?"

"No one would have believed me, they would have thought I was crying wolf to get attention."

"What do you think happened to Dustin?"

"I think he might have been was molested but I don't think by my Dad."

"Who then?"

"I don't know but I'm sure my dad knows."

Jeremy looked from Allison to captain Johnson. The captain got out of his chair and excused himself from the office, he went to Phyllis and whispered in her ear. She handed him Henry and ran out of the office. He returned with Henry in his arms.

"What a cute puppy, can I hold him?" Dalana asked.

"Sure." Captain handed her over, Henry was happy to have a new friend. He liked her and Allison knew that animals had the instinct to know who they could trust and who they couldn't Henry trusted her and Allison knew that Dalana was not a killer, the only thing she was guilty of was faking her death and no one could blame her for that when she thought her life was in danger. The poor girl had a hard life and a hard past few years she deserved some peace of mind and they would have to give it to her.

Phyllis returned and handed the captain a piece of paper.

"Thank you Darling." She smiled at her new husband and then turned to Dalana, Henry had fallen asleep curled up on her lap.

"Can I hold him a while longer?" She asked Phyllis.

"It's fine with me." She told her before returning to her post.

"What's that?" Jeremy asked referring to the paper that Phyllis had brought in.

"I had the Mrs. Go across to the court house and persuade the judge to put a rush on the warrant." He handed it to Jeremy. "You get some uniforms and search that house top to bottom."

"I'd like to help." Sampson said.

"No, your too involved in this case as it is son, you better just stay put."

"Ok, but I have to ask, do I still have a job?"

"Young man you have done some things that are definitely against the rules but I have no intention of firing you for it, I guess I'm getting soft in my old age."

"In Bobby's defense Captain, he begged me to come forward he asked me to trust him, and you but I just wasn't ready, I should have listened to him."

"What's done is done young lady you are here now that has to count for something."

"Thank you captain."

"I can't make any promises beyond my power but I will put in a good word and do what I can to make sure that you stay on the force."

"That's all I can ask for Sir."

"We better get moving, If Tom Gamble knows something is up he will run."

Allison could sense that something was not right in McFarland and they still had a thirty minute drive to get there, she paced while she waited and finally Jeremy returned with four uniformed officers in tow."Ok Cap, got my guys and called McFarland PD they will meet us there and make it all legal, we are ready to roll."

Allison headed for the door, he grabbed her by the arm and pulled her back. "Are you sure you want to do this?" He asked her.

"Why wouldn't I?"

"This whole case has disturbed you and I just thought you might want to stay here while we search."

"Don't even think that you are going to go with out me."

"All right then, lets get going."

"Be careful." Dalana added.

"Take care Of Henry for me."

"I will."

They jumped in the explorer and let the officers towards McFarland.

Twenty

Tom Gamble was throwing things from his closet, searching for something. "How dare you let those people in my home with out asking me first, what were you thinking Destiny?"

"I was thinking that we had nothing to hide and that they might find something that would clear my brother, your son of the murder charges that he might be facing."

"What about my privacy? Did you even think about that? I have a right to my privacy my door was locked for Pete sake how did they even get in here? He must have picked the lock—I can sue for that." He was basically mumbling to himself at that point.

"I picked the lock and let them in, you can't sue any one."

Tom Gamble pulled a suitcase from the top of his closet and blindly threw in clothes with out even looking at Destiny.

"What are you looking for in that closet?"

"Nothing."

"Why are you packing?"

"Why are you asking so many questions." He snapped at her.

"Your acting very strange, and I want to know why."

"It's nothing, I just need to get away for a while, away from here away from all the drama, away from all the death."

"I would like to get away from it too but you don't see me running away, I have to be here for Dustin, you should be here for Dustin."

"There is nothing I can do for that boy, there is nothing you can do for him either."

"But why now Dad? Why do you have to leave now?"

"It doesn't matter if it's now or tomorrow, yesterday wouldn't have been soon enough for me. I have to go."

Suspicions put aside, Destiny was now sure that Tom, her father was hiding something. She had already suspected he willingly let Dalana perish in the crash and she suspected he had a part in her mothers death as well, but there was only one way to know for sure.

"Did you kill mother?" She asked point blank.

Tom stopped what he was doing to look at her. "How could you ever think that I would kill your mother, I loved her."

"Ok, did you let Dalana die?"

"You saw that car Destiny, it was on fire, I had to get you out and it was too far gone for me to get to your sister—I just didn't have time." He went back to his packing.

"How much?" She asked him.

"How much what?"

"How much money did you get from Dalana's death?"

"I don't know what your talking about." He refused to look at her.

"I'm not stupid, tell me how much life insurance you got off of her death."

Tom tried to ignore her but she wouldn't allow it to happen, Destiny had gotten a back bone and she was not going to back down from this one, she wanted to know and she would pester the man until he told her.

"Tell me." She demanded.

"Look Destiny, all of us have life insurance policies, if I died today you would get two million because you're the last dependant alive. Besides your brother."

"Is that what you got from mom? From Dalana?"

"Tom Gamble threw a shirt on the floor and looked at Destiny. "If you really want to know what your mother was worth it was one million and your sister you and Dustin, all insured for two hundred thousand. Are you satisfied now it that what you wanted to hear?"

"You still didn't tell me if you killed them."

"No, I did not kill your mother and I did not let your sister die in that crash, I didn't have time to get to her it's that simple." He grabbed up his suitcase and walked out of the bedroom, she followed him into the garage he shuffled some boxes around until he uncovered a safe that she didn't know existed, she watched him pull out a large bundle of cash. "Your name is on the bank account Destiny, so pay the bills as they come in, you have plenty of money in there to get you by for a while, drive your mothers car, I'll call you in a few days."

"Where are you going?"

"I don't know yet."

"If your not guilty of anything then why are you running away?"

"I didn't kill any one, but I have done some things I'm not proud of, things that could put me away for a long time." He kissed her on the forehead before jumping into the corvette and speeding away.

*

"He's running." Allison told Jeremy as they neared the McFarland exit. "He's skipping town we have to stop him."

"Are you sure?"

"After all we have been through you still don't believe me when I tell you something is happening?"

They saw the blue Corvette pass them in the opposite direction on the other side of the highway.

Jeremy radioed for all points bulletin on the corvette.

"Of course I believe you." He told her, giving her that famous grin of his.

"Of course you do." She said.

When they arrived at the Gamble house the front door was wide open. They called for Destiny but she didn't answer, he pulled his pistol and made Allison walk directly behind him so that she was protected by his own body, just in case. They found Destiny in her parents room, the place was a mess, it had been picked through and torn apart.

"Did you do this?" He asked her.

"No, he went nuts when I told him that I'd let you go through the house and his room. He started packing and looking for something, he was so angry that he couldn't find what he was looking for."

"That means there is still something in this room or in this house that he doesn't want us to find. We have a search warrant this time." He handed it to her.

"We suspect your father is hiding a lot from all of us."

"So I figured."

"Allison, why don't you take Destiny outside and tell her the news."

"What news? Is it about Dustin?"

"Calm down honey, I think you will like this news and no it's not about your brother."

She put her arm around the girl and led her outside so that Jeremy and the officers could begin their search. They sat on the porch swing.

"Please tell me Ms. Kramer."

"I met some one today who looks a lot like you."

"Oh."

"If I hadn't known better I would have thought she were you."

"Your talking in circles Allison."

"I know, forgive me. Do you remember when Dustin said he saw Dalana?"

"Yes."

"He did see her."

"I don't understand, how could he have seen her? Unless she—"

"She is alive, she survived the crash, her body was badly burned but she is ok and her face is still as beautiful as yours."

"But I don't know how—I saw the car, the explosion, how did she get out and why didn't we know?"

"It was a miracle in itself that she survived, but she was afraid for her life and she wanted to stay hidden."

"But who has she been with?"

"There is a young man by the name of Bobby Sampson—"

"The creep that always drove by our house and stared at her?

"The man who saved your sisters life, he is an officer he took her to a hospital where he sat with her everyday until she was able to leave and then he took her home to his house because, she asked him to."

"She was afraid of Dad."

"Yes, she feared for her safety and that is why she stayed away."

"I confronted my father before he left. He swears he didn't kill mom and that he didn't let Dalana die."

"Do you believe him?"

"I don't know what I believe any more."

"Your father has a lot of secrets and we need to figure them out."

"I don't want to think he could be a killer."

"No one wants to think it but the truth is that some one has killed these people and some how your father is involved."

"When can I see Dalana?" She asked changing the subject from her father.

"Soon."

"Is she really alive?"

"As alive as you and I." They sat back quietly on the swing, Destiny trying to make sense of the fact that her sister was alive and Allison trying to figure out where Tom Gamble might have gone.

"I think my dad might have molested Dustin." Destiny said out of the blue.

Allison wasn't ready to tell her that they had suspected the same thing.

"When I followed Dad to the garage before he left there was a safe, he pulled a stack of money out of it so he has a lot of cash, He could go far."

"Do you know where he might be going?"

"No."

"Did he leave anything in the safe?"

"I didn't look."

"Will you show me where it is?"

Allison followed her into the garage, the officers hadn't searched in there yet, they saw official looking papers scattered all over the floor. Allison knelt down to pick them up.

"No." She heard Jeremy yell from the doorway. "I told you to stay outside with her."

"Yes but I—she suddenly knew why he was upset. "What was I thinking." She pulled out a pair of gloves and slipped them on before picking up a paper

"Thank you." He told her.

She found three birth certificates for the triplets where the father should be listed was blank.

"Weird." She said going to Jeremy's side so that he could see. She picked up some more papers, they were adoption papers. Tom Gamble had legally adopted them when they were nine months old.

"Did you know you were adopted?" He asked Destiny.

"No, mom always talked about giving birth to us we couldn't have been adopted."

"I mean by your father, apparently Tom Gamble is not your father, according to these papers he adopted you when you were nine months old."

"That's crazy-" But was it? That would explain why there were no pictures of him when they were tiny babies, actually it would explain a lot.

"I don't know what to think anymore detective Lottle. I just want to see my sister."

"We are loading up the video tapes to take with us now, as soon as we get that done we will take you to your sister."

Allison had a vision. She grabbed Jeremy's hand and gave it a squeeze.

"There are no children on those tapes, at least it's not what we have been thinking but it still isn't going to be good."

"Thanks for the heads up."

"Your welcome. what else did you find?"

"Laptop, looks like he intended on taking it with him but forgot."

"He is the same Tom from the e mails to Stacy and Jill." She stated.

"I figured that, he's also the killer isn't he?"

"No, I'm sure he isn't, I have a strong feeling our killer is a woman."

"We obviously have more detecting to do don't we?"

"I wish I could just see it all and tell you who it is but I can only tell you what comes to me when it comes."

"I understand Darling." He rubbed her cheek softly.

"You do?"

"I know I have given you a hard time over the past few weeks but you have stuck it out with me you're a great woman and I'm sorry for the times I ever doubted you.

"I'm sorry I kicked you that day in the office." Jeremy winced at the thought of that goose egg on his shin.

"That hurt."

"But you can't deny that you deserved it."

"I could deny it but I was really an ass to you and I did deserved it." She laughed.

"Want to know something else?"

"What?" She asked.

"I think that was the exact moment that I fell in love with you." She did a double take.

"You love me?"

"I do. I love you Allison Kramer."

Twenty-One

Officer Nelson slammed the trunk lid down after putting the last box of videos into the trunk of his police cruiser. Jeremy secured the Gambles house before climbing into the explorer with Destiny sitting in the back seat and Allison waiting for him in the front. It seemed like it took forever to get back to Bakersfield. Destiny still in disbelief of her sister being alive.

As they pulled up into the parking space it was obvious that Destiny could hardly wait to get inside. Jeremy sent Allison ahead with Destiny while he helped unload the evidence.

"What do think is on all of this video?" Officer Nelson asked.

"I think we will find out soon enough, if we ever get it unloaded and into the evidence room." Jeremy told him.

"I get it, that's your way of telling me to shut up and move it."

"You got it."

They hustled getting the boxes inside so that they could start processing the evidence. Jeremy was hoping to make it in time to see how well the home coming went but he was afraid he was going to miss it. He would love to see the look on those girls faces when they saw each other.

Allison led Destiny into the station, she could feel eyes following them all the way to Jeremy's office where Dalana and Bobby sat, waiting patiently for them to return.

As soon as Destiny saw her sister she stopped, it was if her feet had suddenly turned to lead. She willed them to move forward but they refused. Dalana rose from her seat and stood in front of her sister, they embraced. For the longest time they said nothing, just Held one another.

Destiny pushed her sister away from her so that she could look directly into her eyes.

"Why did you let us think you were dead? didn't you know what that would do to mother?"

"I thought I was in danger. I didn't trust Dad."

"Well, he isn't our Dad."

"What are you talking about?"

"Detective Lottle found the adoption papers at the house. Tom Gamble adopted us when were nine months old."

"No wonder he didn't like me—and he liked you in a way he shouldn't have."

"I wish you wouldn't say that, it makes me ill." Destiny thought back to that morning when Tom had walked in on her during her bath.

"I'm sorry." Dalana apologized. She patted the chair next to her urging her sister to sit down. She did.

"I guess I have to thank this guy for taking care of you the past few years." She gestured to Bobby Sampson.

"It would be nice. He has been very good to me."

"Well then, I thank you. But I am still not over the fact that you kept it a secret from us all this time." She stood up and hugged the young man.

"I did what she asked me to do."

"Did you think it was the right thing? I mean really, did you think it was right that her family and friends believed she were dead?"

"It didn't matter what I thought Destiny, I love your sister and I did what she asked, it's that simple. I'm sorry if you don't approve."

"In Bobby's defense once again, He asked me to come to the police and tell the truth but I begged him not to, I didn't want to come home and I knew if they knew I were alive they would make me go home, I saw the look in Dad's eyes when that car went up in flames, I think he halfway smiled at the idea of my dying in that car."

"He swore to me only hours ago that he didn't let you die on purpose."

"And you believe him? He didn't even tell us that he wasn't our real father. By the way do we even know who that might be? Was it listed on our birth certificates?"

"No, the fathers name was blank."

"Great, and now that Mom is gone we will probably never know who our real father is."

"You were in Rustling winds the night mom was killed." Destiny stared hard at her Sister, wagging a finger at her.

"Yes."

"They let you in because they thought you were me."

"Yes, they didn't question it."

"Dustin was terrified, when I showed up that morning, he thought I was you. Did you hurt him.?"

"I did not hurt him, why would I?"

"Well you have to admit you weren't very kind to him growing up."

"I'll admit that, and I am so sorry for treating him the way I did, and you. I was so jealous of you."

"But why?"

"Every one liked you more, especially Dad-Tom, who ever the hell he is. I know it was childish and petty."

"You have obviously grown up a lot since you've been away."

"I have, I went to Rustling winds because I needed to see Mom and Dustin, I needed to tell them that I was sorry."

"Did mom talk to you?" Destiny had remembered some one saying that Vanessa had started talking again shortly before her death.

"She knew it was me the instant she saw me Destiny, She talked to me. I told her that I was coming back to her and I would take her home soon."

"That's not going to happen now is it?"

"No, because some one took her away from us. I took her away from you by pretending to be dead and now some one has taken her away from all of us, forever."

"Detective Lottle and Ms. Kramer are working on that, they will find out who the killer is."

"You Don't think it was Dustin?" Dalana asked.

"I know it wasn't Dustin, the kid has a lot of problems but come on, do you really think he is a killer?"

"There is a lot of evidence against him."

"Planted. Some one wants us to think it's Dustin, who better to pin it on than a kid who's not all there in the first place."

"It's not fair, He's locked up in that Vine Institution when he should be back in Rustling winds."

"Dalana, don't worry, he will be back where he belongs in no time."

"You have that much faith in these people?"

"I do." She admitted.

Jeremy walked up behind Allison who was standing outside of the office listening in on the girls reunion. He put his hands around her waist and squeezed her tight. She turned in his arms to face him.

"What's wrong?" She asked.

"Nothing. How are the girls getting along?"

"I think they are doing as good as can be expected, it sounds like they have both done a lot of growing up over the last two years."

"I bet, more than they should have had to do."

She could see that Jeremy was hiding something and she knew it had to do with what was on those videos they had seized from Tom Gamble.

"Tell me what you found."

"You were right."

"Not child Pornography?" She hoped for everyone's sake it wasn't that bad.

"No—not exactly."

"It's the girls isn't it?"

"Yes, it's the girls. Stacy, Jill and a whole bunch of others that I can't identify yet."

"How bad is it?"

"The man was running a pornography empire right out of his bedroom, It looks like he was luring these girls into making videos and possibly prostituting them also."

"I warned you it would be bad."

"I have to figure out who these other girls are, Now I have to check out the missing person files and see if any of them match up."

"You think there might be more dead girls?"

"It's possible Allison, I can't overlook anything at this point."

"How did this man do this with out anyone knowing?"

"I don't know, most of the videos are dated only a year or two back so maybe he didn't get deep into it until after Dalana's supposed death."

"It doesn't matter when he got into it he needs to be punished for it, these were young impressionable girls who I'm sure got suckered into this by him, or some one else they trusted." Allison got that look about her, that look that Jeremy recognized well by now.

"What do you see Allison?"

"A woman."

"Who? What woman?"

"I don't know. But she is a very strong well established woman."

"Some one these young girls might look up to and trust."

"Yes, And the only woman that comes to mind right off is the Principal of McFarland High School."

"I knew some thing was off with that woman." Jeremy said.

"We don't have proof yet but she's worth looking into a little deeper."

Jeremy still had his arms around Allison when Destiny stuck her head out the door.

"Am I interrupting?"

"No." Jeremy reluctantly let go of Allison.

"Have you found our Dad—Tom yet?"

"No word on him yet."

"I just remembered something that might help."

"What's that?"

"He has some friends or business partners in Paso Robles, I remember them taking him on boating trips a few years back."

"Great, he's probably in the middle of the ocean by now."

"I remember he would go there and then they would all go to Morrow Bay where they kept the boat. He took us there a few times to see the big Morrow Bay rock."

"Thanks. I'll be back." He ran over to The Captain and Phyllis who got on the phone to Morrow bay police, if he wasn't long gone already they would catch him.

"Did you find out what was on all those videos?" Destiny asked.

"We did, it's not good."

"I didn't think it would be—was my brother part of it?"

"No, your brother was not a part of it." Allison could see the relief on Destiny's face.

"What's wrong Ms Kramer?"

"What? Nothing."

"Are you sure? You look—weird."

"I just thought of something I need to tell Detective Lottle." She ran down the hall to find Jeremy. He was back in the evidence room looking at another video tape. Allison stopped in her tracks.

"You shouldn't be seeing this sweetheart."

"I have no desire to see what those girls were doing but I have to tell you something."

"What is it?"

"Principal Kinny and that Karen Stone woman have something in common."

"The Psychiatrist at The Vine?"

"Yeah, you remember the tramp don't you?"

Jeremy giggled, he knew it bothered her that Karen Stone had shown an interest in him.

"I remember her very well." He raised his eyebrows.

"You Don't have to rub it in my face, I noticed how attractive she is and that she was hitting on you." She turned away from him.

"Yes Karen Stone is one good looking lady but she has one obvious flaw."

"And what would that be?"

"She isn't you, Allison." He grabbed her arm and swung her around to face him once again. "I love you lady when are you going to get that through your thick skull?" He tapped her lightly on the head.

"Oh Jeremy, I just don't want you to wake up one day and realize that my life is too weird for you and you don't want to be in it anymore."

"I don't know who the jerk was but he was a fool."

"What do you mean?"

"The man that broke your heart, he was a fool and his loss is my gain. I don't intend on loosing you Allison, understand me?"

"Ok." Was all she could say. She couldn't believe how this man made her feel, she absolutely loved him with all her heart.

Captain Johnson came in wearing a sour look on his face.

"Allison, Kinney and Stone do have something in common."

"What is it?"

"They both were once an item with Tom Gamble."

"Really?"

"No lie, apparently Gamble really gets around, only these days he enjoys a much younger group of women."

"I think we should pay a visit to both of these women." Jeremy said.

"Jilted women." Allison added.

"Maybe Dalana and Destiny can help us out on identifying these other girls in the videos."

"Do you think that would be wise Captain?"

"If they know them it would save us time on going through every missing person."

Jeremy thought for a minute before making the decision to let the girls see if they could identify the other possible victims. "All right, you can bring them in while I go talk to Principal Kinney and Ms. Stone."

"Not with out me your not." Allison told him.

"I didn't expect to go without you." He kissed her on top of her head taking in the sweet smell of her lilac shampoo.

"Fine, I'll get Sampson to help me out on this end."

"Do you think that's a good idea Cap? He is kind of personally involved."

"I don't think it matters at this point, what harm can he do if he doesn't leave the building?"

"Whatever you think Cap."

*

Destiny and Dalana were still playing catch up in Jeremy's office.

"I was made head of the cheer leading squad." Destiny told her.

"I know." Dalana admitted.

A look of realization came over Destiny's face.

"You're the reason I got the boot aren't you? You pretended to be me."

"Yes." Dalana waited for the repercussions of her action.

"It doesn't matter, I needed the wake up call anyway."

"Your not angry with me?"

"Yes I'm angry with you, you pretended to be dead, you impersonated me-I should strangle you."

Bobby and Dalana were taken aback at her choice of words.

"Oh sorry! Bad choice of words. But with that said I forgive you and I want us to start over being the sisters that we should have been all along."

"I can do that." Dalana told her.

"Good."

"Sorry to interrupt girls, Allison and I have to go interrogate—I mean interview some people."

"Are we free to go?" Bobby asked.

"Not exactly, Cap wants you to help go over evidence and see if the girls can possibly identify any of the other girls on the tapes."

"Really, he is letting me work on the case?"

"As long as you stay in the station and keep your nose clean."

"I can do that."

"All right we will be back soon."

Twenty-Two

Karen Stone sat in front Of Dustin Gamble's room, staring at him through the clear glass, he rocked back and forth on his cot. He kept repeating Destiny's name.

"Sorry kid, I don't know what to tell you."

"What do you have to tell me?" Jeremy whispered over her shoulder.

"Detective Lottle, I I didn't know you were coming." She stammered.

"One never knows when or where I might show up."

"Can I help you?" She stood to face him.

"I wanted to check in on Dustin, see how he's doing."

"He is ok, condition hasn't changed much from the last time you saw him."

"Did you ever find out how he got out of his room that night?"

"No, I'm sorry to say we still don't know how that happened."

"What? Ms. Stone—"

"Karen, call me Karen." She insisted giving him a sly grin.

"I think it would be wise not to do that."

"Why not Detective?"

"Because I'm here on official business, not personal."

"We could make it personal." She ran her hand over his broad chest. He pulled her hand off of him letting it fall back to her side.

"Do you act like this with every man that comes along?"

"Only the very handsome ones like yourself."

"Can we please get back to the matter at hand."

"I suppose."

"Do you know Tom Gamble?"

"This would be Dustin's father?"

"I think you know exactly who he is."

"And what makes you think that?" She looked down at her toes giving Jeremy the impression that she might be getting a bit nervous.

"Well Ms. Stone, my job is to find out what people are hiding, and I think that you are hiding something."

"What on earth would I be hiding from you?" She asked giggling nervously.

"The fact that you and Tom Gamble had a relationship."

"I don't know where you got that idea Mr. Lottle, but it simply is not true." She began to walk away.

"Is that it? Your going to stop talking to me now?"

"Is there a reason I should keep talking to you?"

"I could take you down to the station." He threatened.

"Under what pretense? You have no reason to take me down town." Damn her, she was right he couldn't hold her on a hunch.

"Fine, have it your way Ms. Stone." He turned away from her and aimed his attention toward Dustin, the poor kid was so pale and thin. He really felt sorry for him now that Allison had convinced him that he was not the killer, he was just a poor kid who had some tough breaks, and he hoped one day soon things would get better for him.

"I'm working on it kid, hopefully you can go back to Rustling Winds and nurse Sonny soon."

Dustin stopped rocking and looked up at Jeremy.

"Nurse Sonny." He repeated.

"Yeah! You like her don't you?"

"Nurse Sonny." He repeated again.

"Ok kid, try to get some rest and I'll bring your sister Destiny to see you soon."

He walked out of the Vine institution feeling like he has missed something. He called the station and had Captain Johnson put a tail on Ms. Stone and Principal Kinney. "And while your at it put a tail on Nurse Sonny from Rustling winds." He told him.

He climbed back into the explorer.

"I'm very proud of you." He told Allison.

"And why is that?"

"You stayed put just like I asked you to."

"That's why."

"Huh!"

"I stayed put because you asked me to instead of telling me to."

"I see."

"What happened in there?"

"She denied knowing Tom as I figured she would."

"That's it? That's all you got accomplished in there, you were in there for a long time." He looked at his watch. "I was in there for all of fifteen minutes."

"Whatever—did she come on to you again?"

"No."

"Liar."

"Ok but I set her straight and it won't happen again."

"Right." Allison's face was flushed.

He had to say something to get her off this subject. " I told Dustin that I would do my best to get him back to Rustling Winds and nurse Sonny."

"And did he acknowledge that you were even there?"

"Yes, he repeated nurse Sonny's name twice."

"I have to be honest with you on this one, I know that she was good to Dustin and I know that Destiny likes her but I don't think Nurse Sonny is on the up and up."

"That my dear is why I put a tail on her."

"You did?"

"Yes, Sonny, Kinney and Stone are all being watched as we speak."

"Good. Because I can tell you that as soon as you walked outside Stone was on the phone with someone."

"What? What else do you know?"

"That's it, so far."

Jeremy's cell phone rang. "Hello." He got a disgusted look on his face before hanging up the phone.

"Who was that?"

"Officer West, he said Stone just made a call that he traced to—guess who?"

"Nurse Sonny."

"If you already knew that why didn't you tell me?"

"It was a good guess."

"I think it was more than a guess."

"Your right, and where ever nurse Sonny is she has Tom Gamble with her."

"Are you sure—of course you are, it's just a habit that I keep asking, it's not that I don't believe you."

"I know that Jeremy, So where should we look first?"

"I would suggest The Gamble house."

"Really? Why would they go there?"

"Because they wouldn't expect the police to go back after it's been searched. But we have you and you know there is something going on, so we are going back."

"Well let's get on the ball man."

"You got it babe, hold on to your seat."

*

Principal Kinney left the Bank with a much larger bag than she had entered with. No she didn't rob the place but she did cash out on her accounts. She was headed to a place far away from McFarland California and she couldn't wait to get there, she had only one stop to make before she left that town for good.

"I can't believe how stupid you are Tom, keeping those videos right here in the house."

Nurse Sonny slapped him across the face. Tom Gamble would have slapped her back had it not been for the fact that she had tied him to a chair so tight he could barely breathe. One minute he's on his way to Paso Robles to get the keys to his buddies boat, the boat that he hoped would carry him to freedom, he stopped for gas and the next thing he knew he woke up back in his own house, tied up, with a crazy nurse standing over him.

"What did you do to me?"

"Relax, I just gave you something to help you sleep for a while, it will all be out of your system soon enough."

"I don't understand why you're here. And why do you have me tied up?"

"You are so stupid Tom, I am the reason that you have so much money right now."

"I don't understand."

"Of course you don't, who do you think is behind this whole set up?"

"Karen."

"Ok, Karen is indeed involved but you and she are not the only players in this game you dumb cluck, I worked hard to get this operation going and you came along and screwed it up royally."

"I didn't—"

"I don't want to hear your excuses, she back handed him again. You are so stupid, had you not started sleeping with every woman you came in contact with this all wouldn't be happening."

"Calm down Sonny, what's done is done."

"Karen." Tom seemed relieved to see a friendly face.

Karen Stone approached him and ran her hand along his flushed face.

"Oh Tom, we could have been good together."

"We were good together."

"Yes, but you got greedy."

"I got no more than you did."

"I'm not talking about money you idiot, I loved you but I wasn't enough for you, it couldn't just be enough to do your assigned job, the video taping, you had to start sleeping with those girls, you always did like the young ones didn't you?"

" What do you want from me Karen?"

"I want to see you suffer for what you did to me."

"And me." Principal Kinney walked through the door. "You could have been happy with me too."

"Well now Tom, it looks like had you been faithful to Your wife Vanessa all this wouldn't be happening now."

"What exactly is happening Sonny?"

"Well, you are about to be taken into custody and charged with murder, that is unless I decide to kill you first."

"I didn't kill anyone."

"Have you forgotten about those three young girls? That poor young man who happened to be in the wrong place at the wrong time, oh and let's not forget about your dear precious Vanessa."

"I didn't kill any of them."

"Of course not, however the police will never know that." Sonny told him.

"Why did you have to kill them?"

"I wouldn't have had to if not for Kinney, she couldn't hide her jealousy and she confronted the girls, they were going to talk, they were going to go to the police and tell them everything they knew. everything that we had done as well as what they had done."

Karen pulled the bag out of Kinney's hand. " Is it all in here?"

"Yes, eight hundred thousand."

"Good." Karen Stone took a gun out of her coat pocket and walked over to Tom. She stood behind him and placed the gun in his hand, keeping hers over it she quickly aimed at Principal Kinney and forced the trigger down, shooting her right in the chest. She was dead before she hit the floor.

"What did you do that for?" He asked in shock.

"Because she is a liability, she had to go."

Tom Gamble was getting more nervous by the second, these crazy women were going to kill him he knew it.

"Are you done?" Sonny asked her.

"Yes, it's your turn."

"What do you mean it's her turn." Tom struggled trying to free himself, to no avail.

Sonny took a syringe out of her bag and prepared to inject him.

"What is that? What are you doing?" He struggled harder to get free.

"Not to worry Tom, it will only hurt for a minute."

"Is it going to kill me?"

"No, no, silly man. But it will wipe out your memory. When the police come in here they will find you with a dead woman and naturally they already suspect you of being the killer, they will think your just trying to act like you're innocent, they will have no idea that you really can't remember anything."

"Have you forgotten about the psychic they have working with them? She will figure it out soon enough." He never thought he would want that psychic to see anything involving him, but now he needed her.

"By the time that freak of nature figures anything out we will be long gone and there will be no one to blame but little ol you." Karen told him.

"And that would have been a plan that might have worked had I not planted a recorder in here this morning, I've got every word you said on tape." Jeremy had slipped in the front door and heard most of the conversation. He had his gun drawn and trained on Sonny. "Put the needle down." He ordered.

"I don't think so detective." She hissed.

She started to walk backwards toward the kitchen, she was going to try to make it out the back door.

"Don't think I won't shoot you." He told her.

"You will have to shoot me to stop me."

Jeremy shook his head, he hadn't wanted to shoot anyone but it was starting to look like some one else was going to get hurt before this ended.

Karen Stone made a stupid move and lunged for Jeremy. He shot her in the shoulder.

"I told you I was prepared to shoot, your lucky your still alive." Karen sagged to the floor beside the dead body of Principal Kinney. She wondered who was in a better position.

Kinney was dead but now it looked like she herself would be spending most likely the rest of her life in jail. She thought about making a run for it but she was loosing a lot of blood and knew she wouldn't get far.

Sonny was still backing up to the door leading off the kitchen.

"You have nowhere to go Sonny give it up." Jeremy told her, still aiming his weapon.

About that time he saw the back door slowly open, Allison poked her head in and Sonny quickly grabbed her and pulled her through the doorway. Jeremy's heart sank.

She held the syringe closely to Allison's neck. And started backing out the door with her. Things might work out for her after all Sonny thought to herself, however, if they had killed this girl when she first came into the picture she might not be here in the first place, she would be long gone, living out the rest of her days on a beach somewhere. She ought to shoot herself for being so stupid. She should have been more careful who she chose to be her accomplices. They had all proven to be unworthy, every one of them. Now that her plan to frame Tom Gamble was a bust she had no choice but to use Allison to get away and then she would just have to kill her once they got down the road some where. That way the perky little psychic wouldn't be able to tell them where to find her.

Jeremy stepped forward.

"I wouldn't do that if I were you." She told him. "If I stick this needle in her neck she won't remember anything, she won't remember you detective."

Jeremy weighed his options, he could take nurse Sonny down and risk Allison loosing her memory, the memories that they had shared, the ones they had created with each other over the past few months. But how did he even know what that syringe really contained. If he didn't try to stop her and he let her leave with Allison she was surely going to kill her anyway. Jeremy held his hands up in surrender. "You win." He told her.

He saw Allison's eyes grow large, she silently pleaded with him to do something. Sonny pulled her out the back door and they walked backwards down the long driveway. Jeremy watched not moving any closer but he knew that he had to do something quick. He heard a rustling in the bushes next door, he caught sight of a blonde head bobbing around and before he knew it some one had jumped out of the bushes and pulled Allison from Sonny's grip. Allison fell to the concrete with a thud. Sonny was stunned to say the least, because it wasn't an officer that had emerged from the bushes it was Dustin Gamble.

"Sonny bad, Sonny Bad." He repeated over and over. Sonny stabbed the needle at him catching him in the right arm, he fell to the ground beside Allison, Jeremy aimed his gun at the nurse once again. "I will shoot if you try to run." She ran, and he shot, as much as he would have liked to shoot her in the head and end it once and for all he only shot her in the leg to keep her from running. Seconds after the shot rang out squad cars surrounded the Gamble house.

Jeremy cuffed Nurse Sonny making sure she had no other weapons on her person before checking to see that Allison and Dustin were all right.

Captain Johnson emerged through the growing crowd. " Dustin Gamble has escaped again." He looked down on the ground. "But I guess you already know that."

"Some one needs to call the ambulance, we have this worthless piece of trash and another just like her in the house with a bullet in her shoulder, and Tom Gamble strapped to a chair."

"What the heck is going on here?" Captain asked.

"I think I managed to get some confessions on tape, that should tell us most of it, I'm willing to bet Tom Gamble will offer up all he knows if he thinks it will get him less time."

"Do you know where you are?" Allison asked Dustin, squatting over him.

"Home." Jeremy whispered in Captains ear explaining what was supposedly in the syringe he had been stuck with.

"Do you know who you are?" Allison asked.

"Dustin Gamble."

"Do you know who I am?" She asked.

"You look familiar but I don't think I know you."

"When the Vine institution called they said the kid started talking like he was normal, sort of, I guess I should say he started talking in complete sentences. Going on about Nurse Sonny and Karen Stone going to kill his father, that Sonny killed his mother. The orderlies tried to subdue him but he overpowered them and got out."

"I'm glad he did, he just saved Allison's life."

"Yep, the sisters are in the car."

"Bring them out, let's see if he remembers them."

Captain Johnson retreated back through the crowd and reappeared with the sisters. Destiny knelt down beside her brother.

"Do you know who I am?" She asked him.

"Of course I know who you are Destiny, and I know who you are Dalana. What I don't know is why your all asking me silly questions."

"It seems that you have lost some of your memory." Allison told him.

" My memory is fine." He insisted.

"Well maybe so but just the same we would like to take you to the hospital and have you checked out."

"If that will make you all happy." He told them.

Twenty-Three

Karen Stone was released from the hospital and sat in a jail cell awaiting her trial. Jeremy had tried to get more information out of Nurse Sonny but she wasn't talking. So he had made a trip to see Karen. Of course Allison was with him. She was still insecure about him spending any time alone with Stone.

"What do you want?" She asked them.

"We want to know why those people were killed."

"Why Don't you ask the person that killed them?"

"Sonny isn't talking."

Allison noticed the dark circles under Karen's eyes, her hair was a mess, she looked nothing like the professional she appeared to be a few weeks earlier. She avoided looking directly at Allison.

"Why did you do it?" He asked. " Why would you risk your life and your career over a porn ring?"

"You wouldn't understand."

"No, but I would still like to hear why you did it."

"Money—love."

"Didn't you have a job that paid you well?"

"A job, that's it Lottle, All I had was a job. It gets old dealing with nut cases when you know no matter how much you try to fix them they cant be fixed."

"I thought that to be in your profession you had to have some heart, some will to want to help people get right in the head."

"Like Dustin Gamble? That kid is beyond repair."

"No, he isn't. that kid is just fine and he will continue to be fine because he now has a therapist that cares and could see that there was hope for his recovery."

Karen finally looked up at them, when she looked into Allison's eyes, Allison saw a single tear escape to run down her cheek. Images flashed through her mind.

She saw Stacy and Jill, she watched them die at the hands of their killer.

"Why did you strangle those girls?" Allison asked her.

"I—"

"I saw it, there is no need to lie about it now." She told her.

Karen hung her head low. " I was stupid, I fell in love with Tom Gamble but I should have known he couldn't love anyone but himself, I found out that he had been buying gifts for some of the girls he had worked with—"

"By that you mean the girls he had video taped."

"Yes, Stacy and Jill, they were young and pretty and they thought he hung the moon, he was going to make them rich and all they had to do was take their clothes off and pose for his camera, in their thoughts they were doing it just for him, they didn't realize how many people were buying tapes, pictures and paying to see them on line."

"So you killed them because you were Jealous of what they shared with Tom?"

"That was part of it, that idiot Kinney thought if we got rid of the girls

Tom would go back to her, she was stupid enough to believe that, She was the first lover he had after his wife went to the loony bin, she thought he loved her, she was like the rest of us, some one to pass the time with until someone younger came along. She confronted the girls and that's when they found out about each other, they got together and said they were going to go to the cops and their parents and tell them everything."

"Why didn't you just run when you had the chance? Get out before it came down to murder?"

"I had to stop them from blabbing, there was too much money to be lost because of those two stupid teen agers."

"This was all about money?" Jeremy asked.

"I'm sure you have figured out what kind of money I'm talking about by now."

"We have found most of your and Sonny's accounts, we have seized Gambles as well."

"Wouldn't you kill for that kind of money?"

"No Ms. Stone I wouldn't."

"You set them up didn't you?" Allison asked.

"I e mailed them from Tom's e mail account told them to wear the gift I had bought them for Christmas, the lingerie, because it would mark the start of a new life together, they both fell for it, they opened their doors willingly hoping to see Tom but all they got was me, when I saw each of them standing there in their red velvet all made up for him it was easy to choke the life out of them, I didn't feel a bit sorry for doing it either." She admitted.

"What about the others, Vanessa?"

"Sonny had to take care of Vanessa, she came out of her fog for some reason and started talking, asking to see her husband, she knew if she talked to Tom it would be all over for us, the only reason Tom was so gullible was because Sonny promised to always take care of his wife if he continued his operation with us. If he knew Vanessa was coherent he would have stopped what he was doing."

"And you couldn't have that could you, so Sonny killed her and framed Dustin?"

"Yes, Who was Dustin going to tell, he couldn't put a sentence together."

"So you got him to your facility where you would be his doctor and could keep him doped up, is that right? Make every one think he was guilty and as long as he was doped up her could never say different."

"You are correct." She smiled to herself.

"What about the boy, Jim Gunner and Janice?" He asked.

"I don't like blood, Sonny was responsible for them as well, the Gunner boy just got his nose where it didn't belong and wanted in on the action, He said if Sonny didn't share some of that money he would out the whole operation. Sonny didn't want to share any more money with anyone, Janice was about to show you the e mails from Tom that were really from me, we had to dispose of her. Nosey girl that she was."

"No, you didn't, We can trace those e mails and track whose computer they really came from, we would have found out it was you soon enough. You didn't have to kill her."

"What's done is done." She shrugged her shoulders.

"Tell that to the families of the people you killed, I'm sure it won't make them feel any better." Jeremy was disgusted, the women felt no remorse for what she had done.

"Let's go." He told Allison.

"Go where?"

"You'll see soon enough."

*

Jeremy drove up to the front of the Gamble house and parked the car.

"What are we doing here?" She asked.

"Well I was asked to bring you here."

"Why?"

"There are some people who wanted to thank you."

"Thank me, I didn't do anything."

"Sure you did." He walked to her side of the car and opened the door for her. He had to all but pull her out and force her to the front door.

Dustin opened the door before they rang the bell.

"We have been waiting for you." He told her.

Allison looked at Jeremy, she was surprised to see Dustin looking so well and not to mention him speaking to her in full sentences. She was speechless.

"Dustin, you have managed to accomplish what I haven't been able to do in two months."

Jeremy told him.

"What's that Detective?"

"Making Allison Kramer stop talking."

They laughed at her expense.

"I'm sorry, did I miss something? Dustin you are—"

"Normal." He said.

"I wasn't going to use that word but you are very different from a few weeks ago."

"I am, thanks to you and Detective Lottle and my new therapist, I am getting better and will continue to do so with the help of my sisters. Now that my mothers killer is behind bars and my step father is put away."

"He was not very good to you was he?"

232

"He did a number on all of us. I know what your thinking, everyone thought he molested me but he didn't, he did play mind games and verbally abused me but he never touched me."

"Did you know what he was doing with those girls?"

"I didn't know that he was running a full fledged porn ring but I had walked in on him once a few years back when every one was out of the house and found him taking pictures of a girl."

"Why didn't you tell anyone?"

"When I walked in he was so shocked to see me and he got real angry, he said if I told anyone about what I had saw he would cut my tongue out and feed it to the dogs and then he would kill my sisters and my mom."

"And you believed him?"

"It wasn't long after that we had the crash and I thought he was going to leave me in the car but I got out and he didn't go back for Dalana, I thought he let her die to show me that he had meant what he said about me being quiet."

"So you stopped talking altogether."

"I did, I decided the best way to keep mom and Destiny safe was to pretend like I didn't have a clue what was going on."

"So you faked your condition?"

"I thought I had to. Ms. Sonny was good to me at first but when Principal Kinney and Ms. Stone started showing up and they were always whispering I got suspicious and when I heard Tom's name mentioned I knew they were up to no good."

"So did you know when Dalana came to see you that she was Dalana or did you think she was Destiny?" Jeremy asked.

"I thought she was Destiny but she started rambling on about how sorry she was for treating me badly when we were growing up, I wanted to tell her I forgave her then but I knew I couldn't reveal that I was not crazy, not yet. I had to know what was going on first."

"Why did you pick up the knife when you found your mom?"

"That was an accident, I was in shock when I saw my mother lying there in a pool of blood, I knew immediately that Sonny had done it, and I knew that Dalana had been there to see her. I always knew that her death was the reason mom retreated from reality and when Dalana paid her that visit she knew it was real, she knew Dalana was alive and she wanted to come back to the real world, only Sonny wasn't about to let that happen."

"It's my fault mom is dead" Dalana said.

"No, none of this is any of your fault, this blame lies on the shoulders of Kinney, Stone and Tom Gamble and mostly on the shoulders of greedy nurse Sonny who decided money was more important than people, she didn't care who she used or who she hurt."

"Allison is right, none of you should ever blame yourselves." Tony Peebles came out from the kitchen. He shook Jeremy's hand and pulled Allison into his arms giving her a big hug. " I can't thank you enough for finding my daughters killer, I'm still finding it hard to believe that my daughter was a part in a major porn ring, but she still didn't deserve to die over it, none of those people did."

"I'm so sorry for your loss Mr. Peebles." She told him.

"Thank you young lady, I'm just glad you were willing to help us all catch these people, If it weren't for you we might still be wondering and the bad guys would be long gone or worse, continuing on with their productions, luring more young girls into their trap."

"I think your giving me too much credit."

"I don't think your giving yourself enough." Jeremy told her.

"I didn't do this alone you know."

"But you make a good team." Captain Johnson said entering the house and putting a hand on her shoulder. "I think we should discuss you coming in full time and working with us." Allison looked around wondering who else might appear.

"I don't think that would be a good idea." She told him.

"Let me tell you a little secret Allison, I have seen the future of the Bakersfield PD and you are in it." He spread his arms wide.

"Maybe we should talk about this later Captain."

"Ok, but don't think I'm letting you off the hook that easily."

Allison looked across the room at the triplets, they seemed to be getting along great. Vanessa's two million dollar life insurance had been split up evenly between the three of them so they had no money worries for a while and the house was paid for and One thing Tom Gamble had done right was put the house in Destiny's name before he got arrested, so it wasn't seized. The kids were all living there as a family once again.

"Everyone, I want to say thank you for having us but Detective Lottle and I have got an appointment we can't miss." Allison told the room full of people who had gathered to show their appreciation for capturing the people responsible for the deaths of their loved ones.

Jeremy looked at her in confusion. "Where do we have to go?"

"We have an appointment with my family." She told him.

"Really?" He questioned as they got back into the car.

"Yes really, I think it's time that they meet the guy that has captured my heart—she reached in the backseat and pulled Henry into her lap. "They will just love you Henry."

Jeremy's smile faded. "Your joking right?"

"No, I love Henry—but you're the man who stole my heart, I love you and I want the world to know it."

"I love you too Allison Kramer."

She leaned into him and kissed him passionately.

CPSIA information can be obtained at www.ICGtesting.com
Printed in the USA
LVOW06s0900210813

348845LV00003B/241/P